MW00614290

OSNABRÜCK STATION TO JERUSALEM

Osnabrück Station to Jerusalem

Hélène Cixous

WITH SEVEN WORDS DRAWN
BY PIERRE ALECHINSKY

TRANSLATED BY PEGGY KAMUF

FORDHAM UNIVERSITY PRESS   NEW YORK 2020

Copyright © 2020 Fordham University Press

All rights reserved. No part of this publication may be reproduced, stored in a retrieval system, or transmitted in any form or by any means — electronic, mechanical, photocopy, recording, or any other — except for brief quotations in printed reviews, without the prior permission of the publisher.

This book was originally published in French as Hélène Cixous, *Gare d'Osnabrück à Jérusalem: accompagné de sept substantifs dessinés par Pierre Alechinsky*, copyright © Éditions Galilée, 2016.

This work received the French Voices Award for excellence in publication and translation. French Voices is a program created and funded by the French Embassy in the United States and FACE Foundation. French Voices Logo designed by Serge Bloch.

Fordham University Press has no responsibility for the persistence or accuracy of URLs for external or third-party Internet websites referred to in this publication and does not guarantee that any content on such websites is, or will remain, accurate or appropriate.

Fordham University Press also publishes its books in a variety of electronic formats. Some content that appears in print may not be available in electronic books.

Visit us online at www.fordhampress.com.

Library of Congress Cataloging-in-Publication Data available online at https://catalog.loc.gov.

Printed in the United States of America

22 21 20   5 4 3 2 1

First edition

All my affectionate gratitude to,

IN OSNABRÜCK,

Frau Bürgermeisterin Karin Jabs-Kiesler,
Andrea Grewe, University of Osnabrück,
Herr Oberbürgermeister Wolfgang Griesert,
Martina Sellmeyer, coauthor of *Stationen
auf dem Weg nach Auschwitz*,
Martina Dannert, Municipal Library of Osnabrück,
Birgit Kehne, Archives of the Land of Lower Saxony,

IN FRANCE,

Cécile Wajsbrot,
Inès Briard,
Claudia Simma, Annie-Joëlle Ripoll, Fatima Zenati,

*and, naturally, to my mother Ève Klein and
to her sister Erika.*

This book owes them more than I could ever say.

Contents

Foreword

Eva Hoffman

It could be said that Hélène Cixous's memoir *From Osna-brück Station to Jerusalem* belongs to the genre of second-generation "return" memoirs, recounting journeys by descendants of Holocaust victims to places where family members lived before the cataclysm. But in this rigorously reflective as well as intimately personal book, Cixous complicates and deconstructs (the word in this case is entirely appropriate) the very idea of such a return. Rather than giving us a factual chronicle of a geographic journey to a place where one's ancestors lived and died, Cixous's memoir is an attempt to understand how such a legacy lives in the descendants' imagination, and to decode the processes and possibilities — as well as the impossibility — of reaching and recapturing a disappeared past.

Cixous herself grew up in Oran, Algeria, where her mother and grandmother arrived in the 1930s from the German town of Osnabrück, which before World War II held a small Jewish population but which since then has been entirely devoid of Jewish inhabitants. Through fragmentary, often lyrical recollections, we learn that as a child, Hélène loved the sound of German language and inherited her relatives' admiration for German literature. She eagerly absorbed her mother's stories of growing up quite happily in a charming, unpretentious town and admired "that light dusting of amusement" that Maman "sprinkled over tragedy." The first part of the memoir can be read as a moving homage to Cixous's mother and an attempt to keep her much-loved presence alive in memory and in the present. "She was everywhere," Cixous asserts after her death at the great age of 103 — suggesting how deeply she continues to permeate the daughter's psyche and imagination.

Osnabrück itself, through "seventy years of Homeric stories proffered by my mother," becomes a kind of Ithaca or Jerusalem — a mythical place of origin from which one has been exiled and which one must never forget. But going there in reality is fraught with ambivalence. Cixous wants and doesn't want to go. She feels regret about not going earlier and resists the collision between the Osnabrück of her imagination and the present-day reality. Her prose, particularly in the first part of the memoir, has the rhythms of approach and retreat, of fear and desire, of hypnotic repetitions and incantatory refrains.

When she finally does make the journey to the actual Osnabrück, she finds a pleasant, historic town where she is warmly welcomed by an affable *Oberbürgermeister*, or mayor, and a feminist *Bürgermeisterin* who is a recognizable, even a kindred contemporary figure. But she also discovers how much she didn't know of what actually happened behind this innocent façade during the worst of times and how many disturbing family stories were concealed, under "the tender and amoral protection of secrecy," within her mother's and other relatives' recollections.

Family silences are a familiar trope in second-generation

stories, often exercising a disturbing force on the descendants through the very absence of knowledge. But again,
Cixous wants to go below and beyond the facts to understand what they conceal and reveal. In her Preface, she
makes a distinction between the abstractions of "globalized great History" and the "great little singular tragedies"
it obscures from view; and the second part of the book is a
meditation on the movements and meanings — as well as
the terrible ambiguities — of actual history. "History begins
before it becomes History," she writes, noting that the signs
and portents of antisemitic hatred that eventually turned to
murderous antisemitism were already there in 1930, or even
in 1923; and one of the questions that haunt the second part
of her memoir is why some people read the signs and left
in time to save themselves while others stayed to meet their
terrible fates.

The main person through whom this question is in-
vestigated is the tragic figure of Uncle André, or Onkel
André — "the King Lear of Osnabrück" — who went to Palestine in the hopes of joining his daughter and her husband,
only to return soon after in a state of melancholic "indifference" and resignation. The terrible secret hidden within
these facts — worthy of the Shakespearean comparison, and
the allusions to Job that punctuate his story — was that Onkel
André's daughter refused to shelter him, declaring that old
people were not needed in Palestine: a cruel rejection that
eventually led to his deportation to Auschwitz.

There are other stories of particular people, and other
family secrets, almost literally "unspeakable." But Osnabrück also holds more concrete evidence of and clues to
the collective past. Cixous discovers a *Judenhaus*, never
mentioned in her relatives' stories, in which Jews were gathered before being put on a train to Auschwitz. She walks on
so-called stumbling stones, inserted into the sidewalk and

bearing names of the dead — a poignant form of memorial adopted in many German towns. Most of all, she studies the Book, published long "after," and recording the fates of Osnabrück's Jews. She looks at travel "permits" and other documents that speak of appalling persecutions and increasing restrictions on Jewish lives and movements.

She also discovers a surprising document, listing offers of jobs on several continents, extended through a charitable organization to Jewish professionals and workers at all levels; and she wonders why some people took up such possibilities eagerly, while others refused to contemplate them. In retrospect, the right decisions in such cases seem perfectly obvious; but Cixous tries to understand them from the perspective "before" — reflecting on the strangeness of having to choose among a "superabundance" of potential lives and identities. This was especially true, she speculates, for those who felt that their identity was not only Jewish, but firmly German. Indeed, she discovers a photo of Onkel André with several Jewish friends, and she notes that they were recognizably modern men, respectably dressed, and indistinguishable from other Germans. This, ironically, made them, in the eyes of hate-filled antisemites, only more insidiously dangerous — but perhaps that is another kind of perception available only in hindsight.

If Cixous is sympathetic to such dilemmas, that may be because she herself bridles against the pressure to adopt a narrow, monolithic identity. "I had wanted," she says, "to see . . . where, in what landscape, in what climate, on what occasion or date or season, I had lost, before my birth . . . the rights of the self, the right to be-Jewish and to be-notJewish at will, at my will, whenever I felt like it." But suffering obligates; and Cixous, reflecting on the fates of her relatives and so many others during the Holocaust, accepts her indissoluble ties to the Jewish past. For all her analytic urge to shun facile concepts of Jewishness or historical trauma, this is a deeply felt and deeply affecting book, permeated by a sense of love and loss, and of the desire to enter and understand — insofar as possible — a tragic and complex past.

Peggy Kamuf's translation wonderfully captures the tonal spectrum of Cixous's writing — ranging from an almost contemplative inwardness, to the rhythms of reflective thought, to very concrete, specific observation and analysis. Her task here must have been anything but easy; but she has given us, in English, prose that is worth savoring, and a work that deepens our understanding of a subject that matters to us all.

Translator's Preface

Those who rely on English translations in order to read the work of Hélène Cixous may or may not know that they have so far been let into only a small part of her prodigious oeuvre. Prodigious, which is also to say prolific. Over more than fifty years, the writer has published seventy-five or so major texts, of which one might plausibly guess that only about a quarter of them has been rendered into English. Contrast this to the fact that every available scintilla of writing by many of Cixous's contemporaries and peers, Jacques Derrida, Michel Foucault, and Jean-Luc Nancy (for example and to mention only these), finds its way quickly into translation for the Anglophone reader. Yet it was Derrida who repeatedly affirmed that "Hélène Cixous is in my eyes, today, the greatest writer in the French language."[1] It's true that her writing has been reputed to be difficult ever since her famous essay "The Laugh of the Medusa" rocked a whole generation and beyond of English-speaking feminist theorists when its translation was published in 1976.[2] However, years afterward and not all that long ago, in 2010,

Cixous herself reflected on how this fraught early reception of her writing distorted, at least for the Anglophone reader, the idea of what she was up to and what her work was about. If one read or could read no further than "The Laugh of the Medusa," this induced an idea of its author as a verbal flamethrower, and yet, insists Cixous thirty-five years later, "I am not an *author of manifestos*. Do you hear me? I write. I am someone given to silence, to retreat."[3]

"I write." For Cixous, writing is first of all an intransitive practice, by which I mean that it does not convert written language immediately into transitive objects or referents but suspends referential movement in its own space of writing. There are many ways in which it accomplishes this. The most obvious is perhaps, precisely, the way it spaces itself out on the page, with many blanks, or else in poetic lines. There is also the idiosyncratic punctuation, omitting many periods, neglecting to place commas, with the frequent result that sentences run into each other or do not close. Neologisms and suitcase words, metonymies and homonyms, the space of Cixous's writing is populated and animated by such inventions. To read it is to watch writing live and breathe on the page, as in a kind of theater where the characters are letters and words. This affinity with theater thus bridges two of the most significant parts of Cixous's oeuvre, literary fiction like *Osnabrück Station to Jerusalem*, on the one hand, and, on the other, her properly theatrical writing, especially for the *Théâtre du Soleil*.[4]

As for the theater within this theater of language, the play within the play, it is peopled by characters in the traditional sense, by actions and reactions, by events, which are terrible events, by passions and compulsions, secrets and hatreds. The main characters are drawn from the family of Cixous's mother and grandmother, the Jonas family of Osnabrück, who were for about eighty years part of a small Jewish community in this midsize city of Lower Saxony. After the war, Osnabrück counted not a single Jew. Most had been deported and murdered in the camps; others emigrated if they could and if they managed to overcome their own inertia. It is this inertia and failure to escape that Cixous seeks to account for, in an accounting that must rely on fiction and invention, for, inexorably and by definition, there is no one left to give the one true account of why one failed to save oneself when it was still possible. The main counterexample of this seeming death drive is Ève Cixous, *née* Klein, the mother of Hélène and the daughter of Rosalie Jonas Klein. Ève left Germany in 1929 at age nineteen and lived a very long, full, adventurous, uncompromising life, dying in 2013. She, along with her mother, Rosi (called Omi), Hélène's grandmother, were the overlapping sources of the family stories, the comedies and tragedies, out of which the writer weaves her text.

Yet these stories were also full of omissions and forgettings and were often subtended by a Jonas family watchword: *Il ne faut pas le dire*, "One must not speak of it." This watchword is the second title of a text by Cixous published in 2001 (and as yet untranslated), *Benjamin à Montaigne. Il ne faut pas le dire*.[5] The eponymous Benjamin of this book is Benjamin Jonas, the youngest of Omi's seven brothers and sisters. This text draws out a terrible family secret about Benjamin's fate from under the injunction to say nothing about it. Especially in its middle section, titled "L'égarement d'Osnabrück," one may read the clear outline that, fifteen years later, the present book would fill out with unsparing detail. This titling phrase is altogether ambiguous: One could translate it by the error, the fault, the going astray of Osnabrück, or else by the mislaying of Osnabrück, however odd that sounds (how does one mislay a city?).

Both of these senses have been aptly revived here in

this more recent text. The "error of Osnabrück" is putting it mildly, of course, when it's a question of the vicious antisemitism that hounded all that city's Jews until they either emigrated or were killed. But the city itself acknowledged this "error" when, some sixty years after the purge, it convoked those Jews from Osnabrück still surviving anywhere in the world to return and receive the honors of the city. One of these survivors is Ève Cixous and another her sister Éri, who, after an understandably long hesitation, accepted to go back and be received in the city that had chased them out. All of this is recounted in the book *Benjamin à Montaigne*, but it also has import for *Osnabrück Station to Jerusalem* because the author-narrator Cixous is herself going to Osnabrück, her mother's native town, for the first time, but thinking as she does so of Ève's and Éri's return there and seeking to imagine how their experience would have been haunted by so many ghosts. She thus goes there ostensibly without her mother, who had died a few years earlier, yet discovers it is impossible to go there for the first time, since all her life she heard stories of Osnabrück, Osnabrück, Osnabrück, from the three fates, Ève, Omi, and Éri. Going to Osnabrück without her mother and her grandmother and all the rest is impossible; they accompany the journey like Dante's Virgil through the circles of hell.

As for the sense in which Osnabrück has not only gone astray but been mislaid, this fault, if it is one, would redound to the author-narrator who, in 1999, published a text titled simply *Osnabrück*, in which, more or less for the first time but certainly not the last, she turned her writing over to associations with her mother going back to earliest childhood, zigzagging through her ambivalence especially after the death of her father when she was eleven, evoking the repeated scene of Ève's narration of her own girlhood in Osnabrück, up to the book's conclusion, when the author-narrator registers her wish to want to go to Osnabrück with her mother: "—I should go once to Osnabrück with Maman to Osnabrück where I have never gone, I should, I should find the time the desire the station I thought and I tried to want to go there for her birthday." These almost-final lines of *Osnabrück* are quoted herein (4) when the text opens, as if to recall the unfulfilled promise that had been mislaid so many years ago. A few lines further down in *Osnabrück*, the sense of promise is even more pronounced: "—Yes, I say. We will go. We will go to Osnabrück where I have never wanted to go. It is time. I don't say 'yet.' We will be there in the next book, I thought. Osnabrück where there are no more Jews."[6] It is, one could say, this next book that was mislaid for another fifteen years until *Osnabrück Station to Jerusalem*.

As in the rest of Germany and the Reich, antisemitism did not suddenly arrive on the scene in Osnabrück in 1933 with the Nazis' rise to power, any more than it appeared suddenly in France in 1940 with the German occupation and its anti-Jewish laws, which were so vigorously enforced by authorities of the Vichy government. This self-evidence underscores the question that, as I've said, is central to Cixous's text: Why did people wait to leave and to save what could be saved (life, lives), when the threat was so patent, so in-your-face? People such as Omi's oldest brother, Andreas Jonas, aka Onkel André, who died in Theresienstadt. His is the singularly perplexing and tragic case that becomes the focus of the author-narrator's questions as she wanders the streets of Osnabrück while slotting fragments of Ève's and Omi's stories back into the place where they originated. Onkel André's tragic figure is that of Shakespeare's Lear as well of the biblical Job, both compelling parallels, as readers will discover when they learn the circumstances of his failure to escape. But there is also Gerda, who ignored the pleas of her cousin Ève to leave Germany and come to Oran, Algeria, where Ève had settled down with the man she met in Paris after leaving Osnabrück years earlier. Hers is a different case, but with the same outcome, although it was in Auschwitz rather than Theresienstadt. And there is also Omi, who did finally leave but at almost the last moment, in late 1938: The author-narrator continues to question why her grandmother resisted for so long Ève's urgings to get out. These are but three of the countless cases, which were precisely *not* cases but each time the destiny of a singular character.

But what does that mean, destiny? This is, it seems to me, a key question for *Osnabrück Station to Jerusalem*. Destiny is thought to unfold toward a destination, a point of arrival that fulfills life's journey as destined, precisely, to end there, to arrive in the end at the end. But what if this idea of destiny were the illusion cast over the incalculable, unpredictable measure of chance events and encounters? At one point Cixous interrupts her own text to reproduce several pages of a circular that had been distributed in Osnabrück's Jewish community and that advertised positions for emigrating Jews who could meet certain qualifications. The positions range from university chemists to housemaids, doctors to auto mechanics, and they are from throughout Western Europe but also well beyond. By setting this long quotation within her text, Cixous effectively positions her reader in the place of those other readers, the first addressees, who read these announcements with some mixture of despair and hope as they projected themselves into an unknowable future. Here is how the author-narrator imagines this moment:

> Upon reading these circulars, the candidates from Osnabrück are overcome by the ambivalent exhila-ration that is aroused in us at the sight of the "gene-alogical tree" of the *Human Comedy*: innumerable possibilities of an individual or family novel are

offered to them. They see in the distant year 2000
their great-grandchildren working in a hospital in
Shanghai or having rapidly made a fortune managing
a supermarket in Johannesburg, and simultaneously
they see themselves dying of malaria having barely
set foot in Morocco.

Such a superabundance of possible biographies
arouses in them either an exaltation or a paralysis.
                                    (96; emphasis added)

It is as if destiny were up for grabs, its "innumerable possibilities" on offer. And, thereby, it is canceled as a destined,
predestined destiny. Yet in the fated response to this super-
abundant choice, what else but destiny decides the choice
between exaltation or paralysis and consequently perhaps
between a life saved and a life lost? Cixous would doubtless
turn this question over to Dr. Freud and to psychoanalysis
while substituting for the term "destiny" the name of the
unconscious. Just so, she imagines Onkel André, one of the
paralyzed ones, wishing that he could have asked Freud
"why his fears always realized his desires" (84). In other
words, perhaps, why this paralysis? In the fiction, Andreas
Jonas has this thought as he passes by 19 Berggasse, Freud's
address in Vienna, which is padlocked, and this last detail
places him there, in the fiction, after Freud has fled Vienna
for London, at almost the last possible moment in 1938.
Freud, at least, realized he must leave. For Andreas, "now
it is too late."

The English reader must not be too dismayed to find so
much German in this translation. For, as the author-narrator
says to her daughter in one of their many dialogues, "All of
this happened in German" (120). It happened in the German language, Cixous's mother's mother tongue, but it also

happened *to* the German language. That too is a part of the history being retrieved and reinvented here, how language could become "a plague that spread throughout the city" (51): "O sweet German language, supple friend of the poets, you were treated like a concentration camp judeo-guineapig, on your tender cat's body were grafted crocodile fragments, fangs were implanted in your words" (54). Still, German also resonates here in the accents of Omi and Ève, a part of the dreamy soundtrack of a childhood in Oran, where *Kristall* designated not the shattering of *Kristallnacht* but the Bohemian glassware that Omi brought with her to Algeria from Osnabrück. Pierre Alechinsky's seven accompanying drawings lift some of these words from the text, beginning with *Kristall*, and, in thick black strokes, stretch them across pages from where they loom over the story.

Osnabrück Station to Jerusalem ends by calling to a next book, which will be about the journey to Jerusalem.[7] This is the next station after *Osnabrück Station*; in fact, this book has since been published, with the title *Correspondance avec le Mur*.[8] There is no English translation, of course. Not yet.

Peggy Kamuf
Los Angeles, March 2019

Preface

Going to Osnabrück is like going to Jerusalem, it's finding and losing. It's exhuming secrets, resuscitating the dead, letting the mute speak. And *it's losing the absolute freedom to be Jewish or not be Jewish at will,* a freedom that I enjoy conditionally.

When my grandmother Omi left Germany in '38 and joined us in Oran, when a Jew could no longer escape except through a rare chance of History, the Stories of Osnabrück began. It is commonly believed that the great Misfortune struck in 1933, but that's an error meant for the History textbooks. Already in 1928 ordinary antisemitism had become Nazi and extraordinary. And death was the master of the City.

If you go to Osnabrück as to Jerusalem, behind the curtain of globalized Great History you will glimpse innumerable great little singular tragedies, which were kept secret in the quarters of this city made glorious by Charlemagne, infamous under the reign of NSDAP, and raised back up today into a courageous City of Peace and crusader for Human Rights.

If you go to Osnabrück, the Secret says to me, walk down the Great Street, in front of the famous Jeweler-Watchmaker's shop, a hundred meters from the Jonas house, your family's house, and look in the shop windows. Perhaps you will see trembling at the back of memory a board of pinned photographs, spectral butterflies, images of all the people who dared to go into the shops of *Jude*, during the black years. Perhaps not. It's here, beneath the windows of the Jonas house, that Omi used to watch the streets and the squares fill up to overflowing with a crowd drunk on hatred, and banners of the Reich, which gave it the brilliance of a terrible opera, came up to her balcony. The sky above Rolandstrasse was red from the pyre of the Synagogue.

One doesn't know. One thinks one knows. One doesn't know that one doesn't know. By casting (itself as) light, History also blinds. I was blind and I didn't know it. But a premonition whispered to me: go to Osnabrück as to Jerusalem and ask the walls of the city and the paving stones of the sidewalks what is hidden from you.

All the time my mother Ève was alive I wished to go to Osnabrück, the city of the maternal family of my mother, the Jonases. Cradle and grave, city of prosperity and extinction.

—It's not interesting, said my mother. Not worth the trouble.

—Let's go, I said.

—One has been, said my mother.

One has been. Now, one is no longer.

So, now that they are no longer, Ève, Éri, Omi . . . now that there is no longer anyone, and that memory seeks where, in whom, to take refuge, now that it is too late, it's up to you to go, says my destiny, the guardian of genealogical mysteries.

The size of a city is an instrument of destiny. Osnabrück does not offer condemned ones the slim chances of survival that vast, complicated Berlin grants. Here, the entire city is a simple mousetrap. The little mice people have no chance. Not one escapes. Neither the Nussbaum family. Nor the van Pels family. Nor the Remarque family. Nor the Jonas family. Nor.

I ask Omi why she did not take off in 1930 with her daughters. And in 1933? And in 1935? Naturally she does not answer. When Omi asks her brother Andreas: "what are you waiting for in Osnabrück? what are you doing in 1941, and until the train of 1942?" a voice stirs in the paving stones, it's Andreas who murmurs, I'm waiting for death at the Osnabrück Station. Don't touch my ashes.

In the streets, the timid phantom voices carved into Silence whisper: go down to the Ashes behind the Curtain.

I went behind the curtain to reclaim my legacy of tragedies from secrecy. And one gave it to me. One: the *Archives of Terror*, kept, catalogued by City Hall and its Libraries.

I followed the traces of Job trampled and skinned alive in German.

H.C.
September 2015

OSNABRÜCK STATION TO JERUSALEM

*I think of going from
Osnabrück to Jerusalem*

I had ended up *writing* Osnabrück in 1998, since then I feared writing this book with a fear almost as strong or perhaps stronger than the fear of not writing Osnabrück, the city that her whole life my mother had recounted to me, her whole life and my whole life Ève took me to Osnabrück with a hundred stories a year, one passed the corner of the cathedral and the Theater, while running on the paving stones, there was also the story that took us to the Hase, the river that made Ève laugh so much with its name of "hare," she used to run and laugh along the Hare, she peed in her pants and she wrote it in her version that she had laughed so much that she peed *in der Hase*, which is to say *in der Hose*, and that is how literature begins, with a river that runs like a hare while peeing, while joking, while cultivating plays on word on its banks,

first the river, and, over its body the bridge for oxen, Ossenbrugge, which is how the city was called in her childhood. Subsequently, Joyce too was beginning to run *Finnegans Wake*, his immortal hare, at the call of his river

ALP — he the erotic worshipper of the Liffey, she the nymph
of the Hase —

Osnabrück! *Osnabrück! riverrun*

Her whole life, my whole life my mother said Osnabrück.
She spoke Osnabrück, she played Osnabrück. With time I
too ran along the *Hase*. I ran. I laughed. I wrote.

Osnabrück is the book that one could no longer stop from
laughing. And sighing too, at the end, powerless to decide to
finish with these words:

> — *I WOULD LIKE SO MUCH TO GO ONCE AGAIN TO OSNA-*
> *BRÜCK dreamed my mother, I would like so much*
> *to take the train in that-place-from-which-trains-*
> *depart once again and go see once again Osna-*
> *brück Osnabrück Osnabrück.*
> — *I should go once to Osnabrück with Maman to*
> *Osnabrück where I have never gone, I should, I*
> *should find the time the desire the station I thought*
> *and I tried to want to go there for her birthday.*[1]

There are days when Osnabrück is a dream. Days when
I am born in Osnabrück. Naturally I had not been there
yet. I was going to appear there. There are those days when
Osnabrück is my childhood in Oran. I was going to be born.

On Wednesday July 1, 2015, the idea occurs to me that
Osnabrück is this book of my mother that feels German in
French.

In Osnabrück takes her source my mother Ève, this Ho-
mer who didn't do it on purpose to dare.

It has been two little years since Ève left, who knows
where the dream leads her?

It is with emotion that I fly toward O.Ran. The train flies over countries, rolls above France and Algeria. It was so long ago. I *alreadysee* our neighborhood, *Nikolaiort*, our house is still on the main square. Maman is waiting for me. I hasten to join her. But there are clouds. The sky is black, an enormous storm promises damage. And meanwhile there's first the arrival at the Embassy of Algiers. Nothing. A detour. We figured that we would arrive in Jerusalem, we are shown into a large empty room, the time to make us waste time, there is no one. Let's leave. Nothing. Crossing the city without a river, the whole city is ravaged, is it in destruction or construction, I no longer recognize anything, I will get lost, deep within I have images of my childhood. Sixty percent destroyed. From '42 to '45. I am guided. I am given explanations. I end up saying: but I was born here. That's true, but. Maman is waiting for me. How long and drawn out is this arrival that slips away!

It is perhaps a dream-that-does-not-arrive.

I am going to end up arriving there, I say to myself, in Osnabrück, by force of talking about it, by force of imagining it, I say to myself, and even by force of not going there.

—*I AM THINKING OF GOING FROM OSNABRÜCK TO JERUSALEM*, the book says. Before forgetting.

—Noted, I say. Osnabrück to Jerusalem. I see, I say. All these journeys that leave from the height of most tender childhood, and meander like sleepwalkers to the golden depths of the unconscious, one doesn't know if one is going to do them in one day or keep them dreamed for immortality. I will know only once I have followed the book to the end.

I had an illumination: why should I not take advantage of it in order to stop not writing the famous Journey in India? I could leap on the chance. Among all the journeys I have traversed with Isaac, it is the most mythological of the eighteen, the stormiest, the most like a fatal illness, the most rebellious against any attempt at evocation, the one from which one does not recover, which resists writing, like the chants more funereal than funerals eighteen in the *Odyssey* and in the *Mahabharata*. It has been twenty years since I began not writing it and I would not like this Journey to survive me and get away with it as if it had not happened. I would not like this monster to take advantage of my painful contradictions to keep itself hidden in the fiction of the fiction. Enough delay. Next year is now, I say to myself.

—Do you know anyone in Osnabrück? my son asks me.

—A crowd of dead people. People who are very much alive in books. They are waiting for me, I say.

One has never seen such a surviving city.

The idea occurs to me that if I keep delaying my trip to Osnabrück, now that it is me in me and not Maman in me who delays this trip every year, it's perhaps because of a hidden fear, if I managed to arrive in Osnabrück, of discovering that all these dead people, so warmhearted, so *bons vivants*, no longer exist in the city, they are perhaps mortally dead in reality, and then I myself would be but a common grave, an unwritten book, and, deprived of Maman as I have been since July 1, 2013, I would not have the strength to resuscitate them. With what voice to say: Good day Aunt Meta! Guten Morgen Herr Pincus! Wie geht's? They do not remember me. They did not know that I would be born. And Frau Engers and Herr Engers? They didn't either. And neither did Horst Engers.

I have come too late. And yet, I remember, that little Horst, so clever, says my mother, about the day he packed his little suitcase, he was four years old and he left for the station, Osnabrück Hauptbahnhof, and the ticket taker asked him if he had told his mother he was leaving for Berlin that morning and I remember that his mother always told guests "for this pie, I paid — so much," "for this hat I paid — so much." About when the ladies arrived for bridge. And on the table that time there were price tags for each thing, from the damask tablecloth to the little teaspoon with the price and Horst had not forgotten anything. Who could forget such a surprise? An artist, a sarcastic dramatist, that Horst, who would have beaten Strindberg and rivaled Bernhard if he had not ended up as bones of Auschwitz before having written his work. I remember these incidents with my mother's memory, as if it was yesterday.

—I remember Frau Engers, I say. A person who was not a lady, but a woman mistress, a milliner, a transformer of reality into originalities, a liberator. —Pi-oneer, my mother says. She loved Rosi, when they didn't know that Rosi would be Omi my grandmother, without knowing the word homosexuality. Pi-oneer says my mother, she's a woman who works so as to be independent. And right after there was the terrible crisis of '29, Omi paid for my music classes with bread, then no one any longer had enough bread for music, and the City prohibited women from working and taking the pride of bread away from men. No more hats by Frau Engers. So she gave Rosi a hat that Rosi never dared to wear and Omi neither. This hat was naked. This hat remained the unknown masterpiece. "Pi-oneer," says my mother, rhymes with "Prisoner."

One July day in another time, my time, in another book, the idea occurred to me for the first time to ask Omi, formerly Rosi, burning questions, as if I was waking up in Osnabrück and I launched them thick and fast toward my grandmother: god? love? lovers? Wunsch und Lust? Kümmerer? Kümmerin?

—Is this detour necessary? says the book. Can't you keep this scene for another book?

—I'm coming back, I say. I'm about to arrive.

That's the problem: arriving. Managing to arrive at Osnabrück. It's like arriving in Jerusalem . . .

One cannot manage to arrive in Osnabrück except by passing by way of the hallucination of arriving in Jerusalem, it's the same, and vice versa.

Impossible to go there without the help of phantasms, a fantastic help naturally, thus not without the help of literature, of its many indomitable horses and its boats animated with desires and tremblings.

For fifty years I was able to think that I would never go to Osnabrück, that in the end I would never have gone there. Even though I always wanted to go to Osnabrück.

I thought, for just as long a time but another one, that I would end up never going to Jerusalem where I could not want to go, where I could not not want to try to go.

I spent fifty years drifting at sea very close to infinitely far from a City, from a coast, veiled, from a Visage, no, I meant to say *Rivage* [shore], Veil, *Virage* [bend], getting farther away while thinking I was approaching, mistaking flight for desire, failing my prayers, saying one word for another, and

I find that I am in the state of the hunter Gracchus, when he was in the state of Ulysses, pioneer for literature, attached to his bark and disembarking for years in all sorts of places, while saying to himself each time *I should one day arrive at my point of departure*. And everything always happened as if the traveler had said to himself in secret: may I arrive

as late as possible

It's like managing to arrive in Osnabrück while managing not to have arrived there.

—Explain yourself, says my son

But during all this time when the traveler follows the book that writes him, he does not read it, he does not know

How to explain that?

—With the *théorie des tresses*, braid theory, says my son.

I wrote "dis-tress" and I listened.

—There is a journey that could be done very quickly but that is delayed, says my son

I imagined Ulysses arriving in Ithaca that very evening, Freud arriving right away at the Acropolis. As if Athens were Rome and he the double emperor. The hunter Gracchus arriving in Riva after having drifted for fifteen hundred years, and the mayor, *der Oberbürgermeister* not saying to him: no Mr. Gracchus, "you have not arrived," on the contrary saying: "Make yourself at home." It's up to you to feel you are in Jerusalem in Riva.

—A train for Athens. A boat for Jerusalem. Apparently you have only a little way left to go in order to arrive. Except that the progress does not happen only in space. It happens in history. Says my son. By dint of turns and generations the threads have become braided, Rosi, Ève, Omi, Hélène, Ève, Omi, Hélène, Rosi, they keep memory twisted. To manage to arrive in Osnabrück and *unknot* the thread, one must redo the whole history that is to say undo so as in the end to take freely the last step that

—Un-knot, *dé-noue, dé-nous*, un-do us, I say. The trip to Osnabrück, I say, what made it fascinating for me is that it was not my trip, it was my mother's, which came down to me in inheritance.

Who remembers now Frau Engers who said the price of each thing and each being? She was of Dutch origin. Afterward, when Ève had become my mother, she got into the habit of saying to me: "What do you think of my new saucepans?" Mrs. Engers having taken refuge in Ève. "Do you know what they cost me?" And I took up the role of Horst, I used to put fake prices everywhere, I made fake bargains, I laughed at the mania of my mother, the most generous woman in the world, which was the mania of Frau Engers, the most generous woman in the world. The least expensive possible, the most expensive possible, and the expensive object acquired a greater and greater price until it became priceless. Frau Engers loved Rosalie, called Rosi, who was, long before she was my grandmother, a woman with a dazzling gaze, whose steely blue will have caused carnage. War widow. *Schade*. You kill me, thinks Frau Engers, Rosi, Rosi, you flay my heart. You can take my husband, she says. It is my pleasure. You don't owe me anything. You gave me your friendship. I lend you my Freerk. Preferably on Fridays. And this is how Rosi broke the fast. And I inherited the well-calculated joyful freedom of Frau Engers.

To conclude, one can refer to page 163 of the book of the Jews of Osnabrück:

Stationen Auf Dem Weg Nach Auschwitz
Entrechtung, Vertreibung, Vernichtung

Juden in Osnabrück 1900–1945
Peter Junk, Martina Sellmeyer
Rasch Verlag Bramsche
Herausgegeben von der Stadt Osnabrück 1988

According to my mother the Engers had left Osnabrück for Amsterdam after 1938, according to her they thought they would be safe with their friends, the van Pels from Osnabrück in a house they shared with the Frank family. I don't know how and when my mother learned that the thread of the Engers' story seemed to have crossed with a thread of the Franks', which had crossed with a van Pels thread. My gaze followed their backs, with their suitcases at the Osnabrück station. When they disappeared. Why didn't I ask my mother for all the explanations? I asked later in the story.

—Certain narratives don't require explanations, they shine like a holiday table, one is delighted by the happy moment and one is right not to demand what follows, says the book. For me, everything your mother said will always be true.

And when I asked her if she had known the Nussbaums, and she answered me: "That Felix was unhappy. He was younger than me," that too was true. She was a hundred years old and he died (*ermordet*) in 1944 at forty years old, he had thus become much younger than her since his disappearance. His mother also used to buy hats from Frau Engers

But who can deny that the dead always have a chance to take a little turn in life? It just requires an occasion. An exhibition at the Museum of Judaisms, for example. That day, Ève had just turned one hundred. —Felix Nussbaum, I say.

Ève. —I remember Felix. Is he still alive?

Me. —He died at Auschwitz.

Ève. —He had two older brothers. But he had a gift for painting. He was an artist. The brothers were in America. The parents were shopkeepers. He had stayed because he had a girlfriend who moreover was not Jewish.

Me. —You never told me that. You had to wait until 2010?

Ève. —He was a neighbor, he lived across from us. He went to the camp because he had a girlfriend moreover who was not Jewish. He did beautiful painting.

Me. —Now his work is recognized.

Ève. —Yes, but now he is dead.

Me. —But you thought he was alive?

Ève. —But I hoped. I didn't have a lot of hope

Osnabrück is a ravishing little city in my memory, which is perhaps a screen memory.

When I was little it was little and sweetly scented and peopled with tens of thousands of Jews. Under Omi there were still only 17,000 inhabitants but not long after there were 165,000 inhabitants. At 100,000 inhabitants Osnabrück had become Grossstadt. It was a Big City but small. In 1988 I learned (in the book cited) that it had about 450 or 500 Jews depending on the year and not more during my mother's time. And zero at the end of the war. Zero, that's enormous, and according to the Nazis, too much, an innumerable number.

But numbers change nothing about affection, says my daughter

IT HAD BEEN A LONG TIME SINCE OSNABRÜCK WAS WITHOUT JEW, there were zerojews in the charming streets and around the solid, square body of the cathedral of Zerosnabrück, the city was always clean and tidy, if there was garlic at the market it had been heil and quit of Jews for decades, when the members of the city council voted unanimously, its Oberbürgermeister and its four mayors and mayoresses — for Osnabrück has changed a lot, the City has become feminist, it has always been with the times — the return of its Jewish inhabitants, if there were still any around the world, or if not, if the return of Jews originally from Osnabrück proved impossible, then one would have recourse to a transplant, it was time to be done with the ghostly and therefore sterile population and to repopulate through living reincarnation the premises, coats, furniture, streets, and forests with tangible Jews the whole organism of Osnabrück, Osnabrück has always been among the first cities in Germany to adopt new developments, it's in the living archive of the City where

the governing kings, emperors, queens, ministers, marshals
had the idea to predict Europe on the occasion of the signing of the treaty of Westphalia, a peace treaty as extraordinarily memorable as the treaty of understanding between
Job and God, and especially the staging of the signing of
this treaty, of which all the stagings of later treaties are only a
copy.

So the City launched an invitation, no, invited, all the
Jews of Osnabrück still living anywhere in the Universe, to —

—here it's necessary to add the capital discussion about
the choice of the right least wrong word to send to the addressees throughout the world, would it be to: come, come
back, return, go, sojourn, visit,

a discussion during which all the mayors thought they
remembered the thousands of discussions about words that
took up city hall sessions during the very old times when
people were counted in Osnabrück beginning with the
Catholics then the Protestants then the Jews

And what if there was no Jew and thus no response? Coming from the world, coming back, revenant.

In a second moment, in that case, the City would not
hesitate: recourse would be had to a reinsemination of Jews.
But that was the great unknown, they think about it without
lingering over it and they tell no one about it.[2]

There were seven responses, including those of Ève and
Éri Klein, my mother and her sister, and of Fred Katzmann
from Des Moines, Iowa, USA, formerly Friedrich Siegfried K. That's how Osnabrück discovered that it had been
discovered in America without knowing it: it had a colony
in Iowa

My mother thought.

She could not not say no

She could not say no.

She could not say yes

I think

— We didn't go to Synagogue, says my mother.
  — We're not obliged to go, says my aunt.
  — If the Oberbürgermeister invites us to go? says my
mother.
  We say we've already been, says my aunt. As for me, I
want a room at the five-star Walhalla. I want to eat a pork
chop with apples, thought my aunt.
  — Don't say what you're thinking, says my mother

I cannot say that I have not lived in Osnabrück, as long as
and longer than in Oran I say to my son, I always lived,
first in Oran, with Osnabrück, in Osnabrück without Osnabrück, in Oran *as* in Osnabrück. I can say that I never lived
in Oran without thinking of Osnabrück, when I was in high
school in Oran, I was my mother's age when she was at the
Gymnasium, I used to look out the window, I saw that there
was no snow, by force of seeing there was no snow, by force
of not seeing and not seeing snow that I had never seen, by
force of making the word snow melt in my mouth, and of
imagining tasting its unknown taste of whipped cream, the
snow ended up falling from the sky, and I saw it, although
I am not sure that I didn't make it fall in a dream, I am
not sure, didn't I see my mother rise up at the end of the
high school driveway standing on her skis as in a dream, in
truth there were delectable moments when I became Ève.
With time I too used to run along the Hase.
  In Oran there was no river and no snow. That leaves total
freedom to invention.
  Perhaps in the end I was in Osnabrück only to verify that
I had always invented true.

We are looking at a photo. For me, I say, it is The Photo. One cannot say it is a photo, I say to my son. It is Ève's grandmother in person, the archdivinity of the Jonas family. You, you look at her, and she, *she sees you*, I say. Frau Helene Jonas geborene Meyer. —Did you know her? says my son. —Yes, I say. She didn't leave the house, in the last years. She commanded from the window. She was always seated in that armchair until she was fixed in her majesty for generations and generations. She had the first telephone in Osnabrück. Her sons gave it to her. In 1920 there was still only one telephone in the city, and it was hers. She knew what would happen. —You weren't born, says my son. —I have Ève's memories, I say.

I look at Helene at the window of 2 Nikolaiort. She is not looking at us. She sees. I see that she sees. According to me, she sees the centuries march by. I see this in the brilliance of the gray-blue gaze that follows the march of time into the future. —You see that? says my son. —I see her eyes go from Osnabrück to the city at the end of time. It is this journey of time that fills the old woman with a mischievous gaiety. —She seems to see everything that she will never have seen before her death, says my son. I imagine it was the photographer who was able to capture that prophetic brilliance. —The photographer is still there, on the square, from father to son since 1870. His shop is full of drawers full of prophetic prints. I say. Lichtenberg. It's still the same. —It's as if she knows what she doesn't know, says my son. She dies *Before*.

He puts my great-grandmother in the present, I thought. —Perhaps she knows that it's I who will take her name again twenty years later in Oran. Perhaps not. I say. —Will she have been able to see the Black Storm coming toward Osnabrück and get ready for the carnage? Or else in dream, will she have already seen the synagogue go up in flames with some of her own in the fire? —I don't know, I say. She was

afraid that Ève would catch cold in 1924 she pulled up Ève's
skirt in winter, she verified the woolen stockings. Ève was
not yet the one who would be my mother. She (Frau Helene
Jonas) had all her eight children. All eight of them crowded
in good health around her for the day of her death. It was
good.

What a beautiful life she had, that is to say, a beautiful
death, the last beautiful death in Osnabrück, did she know
that, there was Doctor Pelz who conducted the gathered or-
chestra of the eight children sons and daughters, and Doctor
Pelz was still the honor and the servant of the sick people
and thus of the healthy people in the whole city, the head
of the hospital and the protector of the poor, and right away
after the burial (there was still the cemetery) violent and
hideous death began, but no one had yet slit the throat of
Jewish time and painted in Jewish blood the joyous German
knife, no one sang the song of the contented knife. One
still died well. Soon after, dying disappeared. Each one was
assassinated. *Ermordet.* The fact that murder is going to steal
the death of her sons and daughters, will she have learned
that, when? Certain good things escape annihilation. —For
example? says my son. I seek. I find: the photographer. And
also: Leysieffer's pastry shop, 41 Krahnstrasse, since 1909
the best

—I note the good fortune, says my son. I suppose that your
book will lead to misfortune, after some delay. —Inevitably,
I say. But in Oran, when Osnabrück arrived with Omi at the
end of the month of November 1938, and after that lived in
North Africa during the war it was the beautiful Osnabrück
the *bon vivant*, the virgin, populous, charming Osnabrück, I
loved it and I didn't know. It was the saved Osnabrück

Osnabrück-in-Oran was always as modestly prosperous
and satisfied as at the time of the treaty of Westphalia and of

the House of Leathers A(braham) and B (Jonas). Osnabrück-in-Hanover was on the pyre.

End 1938 only Omi was saved. Brothers and sisters *deportiert*. Then *ermordet*. But this was happening in the book being written in German. In the book of Osnabrück in Oran my grandmother was learning French, her son-in-law (my father) threw himself into German, we tried trilingualism with some Spanish, we laughed. The word *Nazi* rang out in my first nightmares, but since I had never seen one, the dream paints "the-Nazis" as a dense and black forest of teeth the Nazis within invisible and bodiless between the double row of which we tried to slip. My grandmother and I are holding each other by the hand and we run at top speed between the jaws of the shadows. Like two little girls

How Ève and Éri went to Osnabrück is beyond me and it was beyond them. According to me they didn't go there, they surrendered to Osnabrück. They couldn't do otherwise. In total freedom. Without any freedom. Invited. By their own City. Their own City turned inside out, hunter of Filth, as in a dream. In a dream the City had made filth, had mistaken the filth, and once the mistake was brought to term, the City woke up. It had invited them, it wanted to celebrate them, the return of the prodigal filth, in reality as in a dream.

—So, go ahead, Éri.
—I don't know what to wear, Ève.
—So, don't go.
—So, shall I go?
—So go ahead.
—So we will end up going. *Nous finirons par y aller.*
Finirons
Rhymes with *irons* [we will go], says my mother
In French

—And what shall I do with my wig? says my aunt. They will think I am an old orthodox Jewish woman. Must I say?

—You mustn't anything. People can see that I have my beautiful hair and you have your baldness.

To give in to the invitation of the town hall of Osnabrück sixty years after the last time, does that still make any sense, we no longer know anyone, Ève thinks.

What Ève could not not want to find again, I say to myself, was the Osnabrück with its rowdy schoolgirls, the pupils of the feminist Fraulein von Längecke, with its sidewalks painted gold by the April sun, with its slender trees in front of the Carolinum, in their dresses with flowering sleeves, but then she would have to forget the dead woman whose throat was slit by Gauleiter Kolkmeyer, to amnesia it, and then by means of an extenuating excavation she would have to bring back to a wavering and precarious present the age of the nurturing City, and all this effort for a week? to do what? And as soon as my mother left the resurrection would be extinguished?

To do miracles?

And so as to keep silent?

We live close to a being for years, we share with Osnabrück, we believe, a rather high idea of humanity, we cherish Goethe, our vital affection for German literature is interposed between Osnabrück and us like a beautiful raincoat that protects our Osnabrückian naiveté. We believe we know our city and we grow up without suspecting that on the other side our neighbor, vice, the traitor, Satan is growing in cruelty at the same rate as we up until the day when

By force of putting dates everywhere, History ends up no longer knowing when the truth will have begun, the truth

begins before the truth, the event before the event, before the Fire, the fire, and the people of Osnabrück understood long before having understood but they didn't know it, the heart precedes, the brain pretends to sleep.

Yet already in 1930 one spring day a lady cried out that it stinks of garlic when crossing Rosalie Klein my grandmother, on a sidewalk of the Johannisstrasse, even though Omi never put garlic in her cooking, she always hated garlic, garlic was her reason for arguing with Reine Cixous my Spanish grandmother from Oran, garlic separated them, my two grandmothers, like a poisoned raincoat. But perhaps it was in 1928 that the lady stepped off the sidewalk

yet Toni Cantor, Ève's friend, the daughter of the rich merchant Julius Cantor, who furnished chickens, turkeys, rabbits and was fattener to the city, the town hall, and the bishopric, had cried *à la Tonicantor* when a pupil said to her during recess, what have you got there — you have some Judendreck auf dem Kragen, your collar of white rabbit, Toni, you've got some Jewish shit on your collar, and that was in 1923, I remember, Toni sniffed but not fast enough to prevent a drop that left some snot on her nose, shit on the nose of the Jewish rabbit girl and still that was nothing next to the massacre of the hundreds of Julius Cantor rabbit throats slit and hacked to pieces in 1929 "that's what's waiting for you" said the bandit, but he was a madman who should be locked up said the police, instead of stealing them and reselling them, it was to spill blood Julius Cantor thought, and still that was nothing, just rabbits in the place of Jews, rabbits yes it was like that in 1924 it was already 1933 that is to say in 1938 that the Kristallnacht fire was lit beneath the synagogue and *Dreck* was already the synonym for Toni and Ève in the courtyard of the Gymnasium.

I will always wonder what became of Fraulein von Längecke, how did she die? a woman in advance, by at least a century, a socialist humanist, she didn't marry, women teachers were not supposed to have a sex life, how was she killed, right here I make a monument of white paper

to the memory of Fraulein von Längecke forgotten and re-trieved from oblivion

This is the cock-for-Asclepius that my mother was unable to pay for before she died.

OSNABRÜCK, IT'S LIKE FOR JERUSALEM

I was seated in the second green armchair beneath the canopy of strawberry trees as I do every summer, the garden does not change, unlike the City, trees are pruned, foliage grows back, the cradle of green does not get old, that helps writing, past years and years not past have embraced, and 1940, 1990, and 2016 have made no more than one summer on the page. Maman and I were all of a sudden acquitted of age. Maman was installed in her armchair, the first one, beneath her cap. I suspected as much: I had made tea for two. It is the first time she has come back to take her place since our Terrible Separation two years ago. I am relieved. I was suffering so much from her death. If she had been alive she would have said "la mort ça mord" [death stings], but she was no longer rhyming, I was no longer laughing at her doggerel, I had ended up believing she would never again resuscitate, I had a deep scratch on my right hand that opened its mouth and spit out a stream of light red blood as soon as I reached for the pen. It was Friday 26 June and she was everywhere.

I will never be cured, I was thinking, I am sick from Maman's death, I am dead, I will die of it, I am abandoned by love and robbed of magic. Job I am, and all the time I have left to crawl will be nothing but a continual lamentation. Thought I. I was drowning. I came back up. I said: Ma-Man out loud. And I went back to drowning.

Then, inexplicably, Maman was sitting in her armchair, it was a day in June, and not only was she in the armchair and wrapped in her bathrobe, which I had been careful to do three years ago, but she was everywhere, she came out of the kitchen pausing before the oleander, she opened the French door to the south, she was on the balcony to the east and she was reading *Colonel Chabert*, the last book I had proposed to her and that she didn't have time to finish. I understood that she was the air I breathe.

—So did you end up going? said Maman. To Osnabrück?

Oh! How much I adored tasting the somewhat acrid honey of her voice! That light dusting of amusement that she sprinkled over tragedy.

So I said: —Yes, I ended up.

—So, tell.

—The journey to Osnabrück, what is fascinating, I say to my son, is that it was not *my* journey, it was my mother's journey, to which is added her sister (Éri) and her mother (Rosi, called Omi). When they went there — thus gave in, returned, came back — crablike, sideways, holding themselves a foot off the ground, I didn't go, because it was *their* journey, their moment of judgment, one cannot perish, pay, rot, sweat, tremble for the other. Once they had gone and come back,

but, as I expected, not come back naked, not naked, as Osnabrück had perhaps seen them, but dressed again, and rather decided to "shut their mouths" as they said to each other but in German, *Halt dein Maul,* not because they were giving each other the order in front of me, but because they had picked that up in Osnabrück,

I was able to take up again my descendant's dream, the oldest of my dreams, the one that I began to caress in Oran, when I had my first dreams of dreams. I have always known that I was destined to want to compare dreams to reality, so as to confound reality, to make it confess its hidden dreams, and that it depended on me, on my visit, on my questions, to exit from its sleep and reveal itself.

Osnabrück it's like for Jerusalem: one must go there, one must present oneself before its faces, one must let it speak and advance toward its language as before the monster Behemoth about which God boasts to Job, one must touch it with one's fingers, one's feet, one cannot know them from a distance

it's like for the sea: even from two yards away one doesn't know it, one must throw oneself into its arms yelling

Now that you have made your journey, it's my turn to go there with you. Said I to my mother and her sister, returned from their Journey to Osnabrück, I say to my son. Finally we could go to Jerusalem, that is to say, Osnabrück! We'll all go together, I say. The dead like the living. I will reserve the Walhalla, naturally, it is the best hotel. We will go by train as it is said in Ève's dream as I wrote in *Osnabrück* the book.

Next year—comes, the moment nears. I say. Ève says to me: we are not going. Éri doesn't want to go.

—But you? I say

—One has already been, says my mother

We went there

It's not necessary

It's not interesting

—So you're not going? I insisted.

They ended up by saying to me: "One has already been," I say to my son.

But in the last chapter of Osnabrück it is said:

—*What if we went to Osnabrück? I say precipitously. Right away a force I had not seen pushed me toward her. I bent my head above hers. For a brief instant we saw our two mouths very close up, and that there was a chance they would*

*touch, and veering off just in time, we nose kissed, I touched
her nose with the end of my nose and we rubbed noses.*

*—Mydaughter! she pulled back her somewhat delighted
face. To Osnabrück? We will go?*

*—Yes, I said. We will go. We will go to Osnabrück where I
have never wanted to go. It is time.*

*—One takes the train from the East station and one travels
all night, says my mother, the words were coming, her dead
were getting ready to meet us, her eyes were shining.*[3]

You have read this chapter, I insisted.

—You have always had a lot of imagination, says my mother.
You invented me. You write and take your inventions for
reality.

You write that I take the train from the East station.

—The train, I say, is to please you. I prefer the plane.

—I am not a fiction. As for me, I take the train for Osnabrück from the *North* station, don't lose north!

—You made a mistake? says my son.

—I think I wanted to make a play on words à la Ève. East
is East, I say.

—One has been, says my mother. She does not say: we
went there.

—One ended up not going, I say.

—This doesn't end, says my son.

—I couldn't go without them, I say. I was thinking of it,
but with bad thoughts. Thoughts of death. "Without them"
as if I thought: you have been, and now you are no more.

After. After, they were no more. Omi, Éri, Ève, they have
been. Now they are in the books. I should perhaps have writ-

ten "North station," I thought while cutting the last pages of
Osnabrück with scissors.

After Ève there came to me the thought born of death: "I
do not want to die without having been to Osnabrück." But
why? I said. The thought hesitated. It was perhaps: "I cannot
die before having been to Osnabrück." Sometimes it said to
me: I must not. Now I could unfortunately go to Osnabrück.
I owe it to Ève, it seems to me.

All the time that Ève didn't want to go to Osnabrück, having
already been there, having done her good-bye, that is to say,
her duty, I can no longer want or not want to think of Osnabrück in reality. I was able to think for fifty years that I would
never go to Osnabrück. One nourishes thoughts with grief
and regret until they become little tragedies.

During that time I remained faithful to my mother, un-
conditionally, that is to say, without explanation. The explanations were hidden in Osnabrück. From afar one doesn't
understand.

—I understood only by going to Osnabrück . . .

    —. . . what Ève used to say? says my son.

    —What Ève didn't say. She didn't say anything. She *just* couldn't return there. She couldn't return there *justly*. One doesn't know as what or who to return there. She was unable to *return* there. The City invited her as a not dead Jew. She *went* there. As such. Such is not she. She talked to me about what she ate: it was *she* who had eaten, after all, not *such*.

—One thing with its frightening word that I learned only over there, I say to my son, is *Judenhaus.*

A city like all the others, founded by Charlemagne, innocent, its cathedral, its sinuous alley of the witches, like everyone, that one day had killed its remaining Jews, as in a fairy tale.

Did my mother know where the *Judenhaus* was
    the house in which the so-called-Jews were crammed

before being shoved into the trains at the Hauptbahnhof, destination Auschwitz?

When I was in Osnabrück I didn't ask where the house-of-Jews was, it didn't occur to me, I followed the street I was looking for the building of the Jonas family, I went up Schwedenstrasse, I passed in front of the monumental Mc-Donald's building, I saw that the McDo's had swallowed up the Jonas store, I had not thought of that, I don't know how many people it could contain, thus six times more if they are piled up, among whom for I don't know how long Andreas and Else Jonas waited for what came next, I don't know what they thought closed up squeezed together in the house-for-Jews, I don't know if they thought I don't know if thinking thought or fled and hurled itself into mute howling, according to my mother, one doesn't think, one repeats a word to oneself, one gasps it, one chews it, endlessly so as not to cry out so as not to be alone with the silence, what word? I say, are you thinking of *god?* I say, no, no, of course not, no, everyone has his or her own, the first one that comes, that passes, a word that answers, that says yes, I am here, I give you my hand, one doesn't think, I know someone who used to recite a Baudelaire poem, a pile of words

instead of think, *feel*, and what does one feel piled in the box-of-Jews, one feels distances of the distances, unknown, vertiginous, supernatural distances between here and yesterday, sorts of centuries of flattened walls of oceans of black waters swollen with rocks, between here and the house where I was I and it was me and all of a sudden there is no longer near, monstrous fars surround the mind and several dozen yesterday-yards mean never-again-Maman-will-never-again-come-back.

no more thoughts, ever, a whirlwind of ghosts

and the use of the past tense has become a mill of sighs

and memories! No! no memories memories are grapple
hooks for the heart, no! no mem

"Judenhaus," that's new, says my mother, it's a word-crime I
say, a word-slaughterhouse, but I don't know if the so-called
Jews knew it, if they understood it with what disgusting suffering whispering what fright to them around the lungs they
learned of their metamorphosis into animal feed

but I don't know the word that Onkel André repeated to
himself, crushed into the box-of-Jews, the name of Irmgard
perhaps? his name of being-for-love.

The following movements of the soul:
    waiting, hoping, fearing, trusting
    are hanged or decapitated

to be the need to urinate
    terror — what one cannot flee
    Irmgard!
    Weh! this breath pain that spreads infinitely, a sea of
brown mud reaches the teeth of the earth
    Irmgard! A solitude, insane, one, who is alone at the heart
of this compressed crowd of solitudes
    — That makes me think of corned beef, says my mother.
You remember? Those cans of pressed beef that the Amer-
icans lavished upon us in Oran in 1942, the year of corned
beef. The taste of corned beef do you remember? I remember the large jar of strawberry jam, says my mother.
    I was doing secretarial work for the Americans. The Ital-
ian cook says to me: *Jam? Biznis*. Biznis? I say. The cook
says: Biznis, biznis, and shows me the bed. So I said: no
biznis. And I left with the jam, says my mother. That was in
1942, the first months of the resurrection of Oran. What hap-

piness, to eat, bread, melted cheese, the future. But it's not in the Judenhaus on Hegerstrasse but in the one on Kommanderiestrasse that Andreas Jonas is dragged, I'm told by the Book of Stations. In 1942 to die has completely changed meaning. It had become the very idea of happiness for Hiob, that is, Onkel André, who before 1942 didn't know he would end up as Job.

In Oran 1942 living had the taste of corned-beef fat whereas in Osnabrück living had the taste of ending, night gnaws the bones of my body, mit gewaltiger Kraft packt er mein Gewand, mit der Kragen meines Leibrocks schürt er mich ein. Er hat mich in den Dreck geworfen, so dass ich dem Staub und der Asche gleich geworden bin and now my soul melts in me, the days of misery grab hold of me I had sisters, but the idea of sister is turned to dust, and my brothers are the same as shit. I am become the brother of jackals and "He" (you-know-who) buries his fangs with all his might into the neck of my twisted shirt, which is all I have left as a body. I am his torn rag, I was Irmgard's Papa in a book back when there were libraries. I was rich like Job, I had a daughter who was worth ten daughters, Irmgard and I used to call her Zuckerkrönchen, I was a man in the country of Osnabrück and now I am as if I had written the first year of a fairy tale hundreds of years ago and saw Satan write the next forty-two centuries with his excrement. My enemies cut out my tongue. Here is the madman who called his little Jewess Zuckerkrönchen, eat it your crown of sugar, cockroach.

Kommanderiestrasse 11, it is at that address, I guess, that the shipwreck of love took place, in a few hours, and perhaps even in a few minutes, that's perhaps false in reality, but here, in the book, no one will contradict it. Without any doubt Andreas had the pain of losing Irmgard in the first horribly interminable minutes following his arrest, and perhaps in the first minute. There are testimonies. Everyone knows that the Ortsgruppenleiter Kolkmeyer was the very face of terror, which is not always the case. You saw Erwin Kolkmeyer his doubles Gauinspektor Wehmeyer and Kreisleiter Münzer, you saw that god had abandoned you or else god had abandoned the fight

Hitler was the one who took a watchmaker and a shopkeeper and turned them into hyenadogs by feeding them on Jewish bones. For his part the hateful hyenaesque watchmaker Kolkmeyer had called his dog "Brüning," he beat him with a truncheon until Brüning would bite all of humanity.

> In place of the image of the photograph of Irmgard
> All of a sudden
> You saw Kolkmeyer and his Brüning
> Is there a prayer against the plague of murder?

The end of love from one second to the next will have perhaps all the same surprised Andreas Jonas or else perhaps not. Still another horrible surprise: instead of the word Irmgard, it is the word Hitler that is recited by the brain.

The voice of Andreas has changed despite himself, it was as if divided, like a forked tongue, like full of resentment, as if under the shock (giving way beneath the omnipotence of evil) all the organs of the incarcerated one had turned black, his reason strayed, hatred catches him in its net, and he goes and bites his own Irmgard in the heel and tears himself apart while thinking he is tackling Nazis.

He lifted the crown of sugar from my head and he buried me alive in the pestilential belly of my own mother. When they killed me in Auschwitz nothing was left to my name but the skin of the teeth of my corpse.

OMI TOOK ME FOR ICE CREAM TO THE CAFÉ MARIGNAN IN ORAN. It was my first ice cream. On her silk dress she had the large diamond brooch of her mother. I don't know what she knows about her brother. Perhaps he remained alive a long time after his death, perhaps he was taken for dead by Rosi years after he became ashes. She didn't tell me: my brothers and sisters did not fall into the same dust, some made dust in the dust at Auschwitz, others at Theresienstadt. The delicate taste of the ice cream is silk on the tongue, the pensive joy of sucking the luxury of the world, Omi's distinction, her person illustrates the word *vornehm*. Was it possible to eat ice cream in Oran? Right away after the event called "landing," that is, paradise 1942, Omi was delicately advancing her thin lips, Andreas was disappearing behind or into the word *ermordet*, if Rosi had learned of it she would not have savored the bowl of ice cream, she would have savored every spoonful otherwise, she would have known

that she was sucking as the sister of Andreas
she would have sucked for him

—Perhaps Omi knew and she did not want to tell her daughter. Ève had worries of her own, having to do with Vichy, in Oran, says my daughter.

—No, I say, she had learned and she said, next we are at the Marignan a chic café that could rival the Café de la Paix and we sucked while celebrating every spoonful

—Perhaps they said to themselves it is too horrible, one must try to live says my daughter,

—It was delicious, I will never forget the scoop of ice cream at the Marignan, I say, it was bliss itself, the divine melts, it is granted to you for a time, you enjoy what disappears, life is short like ice cream,

Omi absorbs the succulence in a timed hand-to-hand, I suck the beginning and the end,

I read nothing on Omi's absorbed face,

it was a matter of communing

time melts on the tongue

some in Auschwitz, others in Theresienstadt, others in Oran

the cousin was in Gurs with her husband, come to us in Oran writes my mother, finally she didn't come, she went to Auschwitz

sometimes between the right choice and the wrong choice it's the wrong choice that wins, I don't understand that says my mother

das verstehe ich überhaupt nicht, says my grandmother, *Onkel Andre hat sich total geirrt*

I don't know. I did not learn what my grandmother learned about her brother. About Jenny and Hete her sisters she learned, how she received the card from Theresienstadt I don't know, it said "we don't know where we are going," the stories sent from the camps are always muddled, their characters not knowing whether to believe what they are sure about and gulfs open up within the family hallways between brothers and sisters are crossed by bottomless gorges. That is why Omi knew that she didn't really know what she knew, for that and for many other reasons having to do with the secrets of the Jonas household sons and daughters and parents about whom nobody would ever know anything in truth.

When my grandmother obtained her unhoped-for expulsion, Osnabrück arrived in Oran like exoticism incarnate. I summarize:

My grandmother obtained her expulsion at the end of the year 1938. She spoke to no one about Kristallnacht. The word Kristall arrived in Oran to designate Bohemian glassware. These glasses were too beautiful to be real. We never drank from these glasses. It was impossible. The glasses are always standing on their shelf. They are full of silence. No one ever dared to push curiosity to break the silence come from Osnabrück.

Omi was in Osnabrück on November 9, 1938?

Omi is composed of the following traits: (1) dresses of shiny silk (2) the word Kristall that she used to designate the Bohemian glassware, arrived with her in Oran. Glasses raised like church bells, melodious luminous. One looked at them. One desired them. They mounted high like rose stems metamorphosed on their shelf. One didn't dare. Once a year — no, they weren't used — they were presented with a little bit of wine out of respect. They were full of an enchanted silence (3) to this is added her German style, an idiom animated by a great number of modalizers having to do with feelings of horror, terror, repugnance, indignation, anger, in passionate sonatas, which transported me with excitement. I used to repeat these furious phonemes as so many synonyms of the storm lodged in my grandmother. I was proud of them. I too wanted to take pleasure in these furors *furchtbar, ekelhaft, widerlich, dreckig, hässlich, grässlich, ent-setzlich, schauderhaft und so weiter.* There were hundreds of them. This was at the end of November 1938

—Omi was in Osnabrück on November 9, 1938? asks my daughter.

—Without any doubt, I say. In one way or another. Be-tween Osnabrück and Jerusalem.

"What happened on November 9, 1938?"

If I asked my mother this question, she would reflect for a long moment. She would look at me with her large brown eyes. She would say:

—It's not my birthday?

—No, no. You were born in October 1910. You are a hun-dred and five years old.

—Oh la la! I am spoiled!

I put her to bed, she eats a chocolate, she's in ecstasy, the flowers have four colors

—What happened? —It's a long time ago. I don't re-member.

I would like so much to have been able to continue this conversation with my mother. When I would have led her to the mystery of 11/9/38, I would have told her, while ob-serving the effect of surprise on her face and in the hopes of gathering up one of those inimitable sentences for which she alone had the secret:

—In Oran, during the night of November 9–10, 1938, you brought into the world a boy, your first son, your husband and Doctor A, were with you, the two men chatted while you pushed.

—That irritated me. You remember that? It's far away

—In Osnabrück, meanwhile, the Nazis first set fire to the synagogue, people thought it was a fire an accidental misfortune, but not for long, because right afterward all the large Jewish stores of the city, and the small ones, were pulverized, the firms of Mosbach, Weintraub, Gossels und Nussbaum, Julius Cantor, Frank, Wertheim, Münz, Flatauer, Andreas Jonas und Miterben, Geschwister Grunberg while you were giving birth

— That's crazy! she would say. We didn't hear about it?

Unfortunately, Ève left me. Too late, I became aware of this fateful coincidence: the night of the destruction of the Osnabrück-world was also the night of the birth of the first son. It was a cloven night, violent, shaken by tremblings. One didn't speak about it. The newborn was not registered on the morning of the 10th. No. He is finally publicly registered at city hall on November 11. No one knows the reason for this delay.

— We couldn't find a name, says my mother. That's why.

— No name for the child?

No name for the event.

The sky was all red above Rolandstrasse. *Osnabrücker Judentempel fällt*

Or else they didn't want to mix up the child and the ruin they feared contamination, the father deferred, if it isn't my father it's perhaps my grandmother

— Omi was perhaps already in Algeria? says my daughter. How to know? Several times, says my daughter, I've wanted to tell you, if Ève doesn't answer one has only to ask Éri. But Éri too doesn't answer.

— I know that Omi knows, I say, wherever she is. Andreas Jonas is also in Osnabrück in November 1938. He watches the history of his life burn. He's the one who tells Rosi the story of the night of fire. I know he tells her while sobbing.

I know he is not crying for the synagogue, he cries for his daughter, in the monumental collapse of the building the burning of the Irmgard memories-images the last time was when?

He perhaps said nothing.

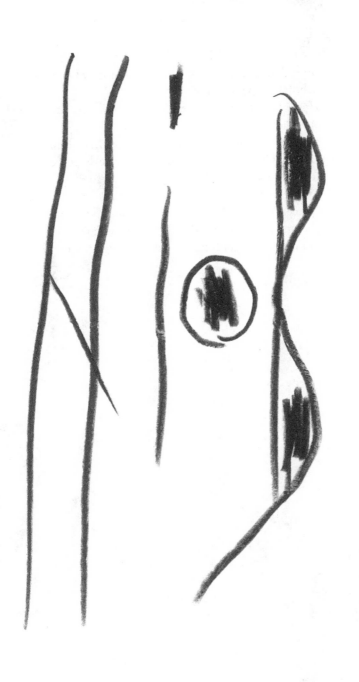

If we can no longer ask Ève or Éri, then we can ask the photo albums, doubtless we'll see whether Omi is in Oran or in Osnabrück, or perhaps not.

How gay and smiling are the women the children the photos like Oran

how far Osnabrück is from Oran, how Oran sleeps in a bathing suit the women graze the babies suckle peace

there is no album of the ruins and the tortures

We are in the jaws of the Leviathan, writes Andreas Jonas, the pieces of our bodies thrown to the hounds that are barking behind the heavy wooden door painted dark blue,

but he doesn't finish noting down his nightmare

ONKEL ANDRÉ is the one Omi talks to me about most often as if her eight brothers and sisters were all contained in their eldest. I note that Omi will always give him his Oran name. Onkel André never existed in Osnabrück. The one who directed the factory and was deportiert in 1942 is Andreas Jonas, the one on the right in the photo of the good-byes at the Osnabrück station, the man with the hat. He looks like Charlie Chaplin. This too I will never know: did Omi laugh so much when she saw *The Great Dictator* because she recognized the double of her brother or the other way around? He too was small, with something mischievous, like him.

Onkel André is the King Lear of Osnabrück. He cannot live without his crown. Irmgard! My adored little crown. When the sugar daughter of his heart married in 1934, and after this marriage emigrated to Palestine, the emigration of his soul began he no longer knew where he was, it was not his journey, he lost his head, he would go to Jerusalem to reclaim his sugar crown, he had a nightmare, he arrived in the auditorium of the Palästina, through the door at the back, the one he loved, his queen, the one who loved him no more, was naturally sitting in the first row he saw her from a distance from the back with her new popinjay, a little blond, he saw the popinjay kiss the one who had forgotten him on the mouth in front of everyone and instead of dying, he tried to get closer to his Zuckerkrönchen, a pain added to an anger which added to a humiliation

what you are you doing here Papa
you should not have come
life is hard here
you are too old
they need young people in Palestine
It's not a country for two old people
—Are you our daughter?
—This house is small. Stubborn parents should draw the lesson from the refusal they bring down on themselves.
—Is it you who are saying that? to your father? Zuckerkrönchen, is it you who are
Sending me away?
—You yourself are the cause of
Your problems. You show up unannounced
Don't look at me like that
Parents keep children in their debt
—Say that again
—What did you come here to do?
You came to help me?
—Say it again
—Or to make me waste my time?

—That's in *King Lear*? says my son.
—It's in *Andreas Jonas, ein Vater* the tragedy of Osnabrück.

—People will think you made up this story, says my mother.

—Perhaps Omi knew and told it to her daughter. Perhaps not.

What does *Stationen*, the book of Osnabrück, say about this trip to Palestine?

—Nothing.

Between two addresses. There is no date, no information. First they are living on Friedrichstrasse. From there, there is departure. Next they live nowhere. The trace is lost. Next they go from no known address to Grossestrasse 44, at the home of Otto David, 1941, Februar 1942 im "Judenhaus" Kommanderiestrasse 11. Von dort . . .

There was not yet an address in Palestine.

Osnabrück-Jerusalem-and-back, months and months without address, *Vater du bist alt*, go back to your sister's, be quiet you are going to drive me mad, *liebes Kind*, I admit I am old, on my knees, stop this comedy, I don't begrudge you Zuckerkrönchen, they have changed you, it's another, go back to my sister's! it's that filthy popinjay who, me I love you Irmgard, worse than the Nazis, how dare you say that! I didn't say it I thought it, it's over, we will never see each other again, I was going to say it, but you are my flesh and blood my little heart, is this going to last for a long time? my carbuncle, my fatal disease,

what were you saying about debt? Say it again. I stop.

Where was Andreas Jonas in November 1938? Somewhere. On a wind-swept heath. She is lost! He is lost!

My body is covered with worms and a muddy crust. My skin cracks and dissolves. My days are more rapid than the weaver's shuttle. They vanish. My eyes will not see happiness again. The eye that watches me will watch me no more. Your eye will seek me and I will be no more. I will speak in the anguish of my heart. Am I a sea or a sea monster that you set guards around me? Ah! I would like to be strangled! I would prefer death to these bones! I despise them. Leave me, for my life is but a breath. When will you leave me time to swallow my saliva? I am going to lie down in the dust. You will seek me and I will be no more. (Job Jonas, 30:16)

Onkel André, says my mother, was the poet. He was the only one in the family who was really not made for business he loved literature. André read Shakespeare while almost weeping. André the one who did not dare. He did not dare say no when he had to marry that Berlin woman who spoke loudly and had a gold tooth. André was very handsome, Selma loved only her daughter Irmgard — Selma? I thought it was Else, I say. — Everyone can make a mistake. André himself was mistaken because he didn't dare say what he loved above all else, Selma adored her Zuckerkrönchen — I thought he was the one, I say. He couldn't stand it. — That is, Else, Zuckerkrönchen! to call one's daughter like that! I would not have stood for it. It's her fault.[4] To go to Palestine! Not to flee the Nazis. I can't tell the story.

And my mother told what she couldn't tell.

— The uncle and the aunt *came* to Palestine, to find the daughter, in a kibbutz that was getting started, she could not keep them, instead of coming to Oran with Rosi, where there are always these moods of sisters-in-law, she *sent them back* to Germany, the expense, the danger, that Zuckerkrönchen, we don't need you here, go back to Germany, have you seen yourself with your hat? Irmgard was capable of thinking what she said, now I can say it, everyone has disappeared, they were deported, she was a complete rotten egotist she amused herself with older men, she had affairs especially with blind men, after that she left, she emigrated, after Jerusalem, Tiberias, a pretty heartless girl, with a crown in its place, she lived well and she was right since she died so young, when she got typhus her parents were wandering on the heath between Jerusalem and Osnabrück and didn't know it.

It's not that Cordelia became Regan, thought Onkel André, it's that she always was.

Who told this story to whom? This story has traveled a lot. Some have believed it, some have changed the names, some have changed the addresses, the dates, Onkel André came back to Osnabrück after a long journey, perhaps he told his sister Rosi everything, perhaps he didn't dare, perhaps it's his wife Else, not Selma, someone learned it, someone thought, someone saw Onkel André accompany to the station his friend Gustav Stein who was leaving Osnabrück forever in October 1935. He thought, and what if I left too, but where, where? one sees him, his melancholic air, to the right in the photo.

For every story, one has another explanation.

> *Everything I am writing here is*
> *perhaps true, perhaps more true*
> *than I allow myself*
> *to hope*
> *As soon as I dress the facts and the places*
> *with flesh and passions,*
> *the truth grows,*
> *takes on depth,*
> *but at the same pace as error.*

According to some the play in question is called *The Tragedy of Andreas Jonas*. For others it's *Irmgard's Tragedy*. According to me it's death and its bag of surprises, the suddenness, the irony, the mockery of poor mortals that will have changed Andreas and his daughter or Irmgard and her father into characters destined for the stage. Is there anyone among the innumerable *people* (the Jonas, Klein, Löwenstein, Meyer, Blank, Seehoff families . . .) from Osnabrück and the surroundings (Hanover, Westphalia) who has another folio of this Shakespearian chronicle? I wondered

This is one of the versions I reconstituted over thirty years: each one is an original, I work on it with the help of memories tangled up by my mother, to which I add all sorts of forgettings, as well as the interesting silences of Omi

The more I advance into human shadows by the light of writing, the more the truth of the Andreas Jonas affair appears to me like a sad and monumental treasure, one of the secret keys to this terrifying period.

It was not easy to go to Palestine, it was long and complicated, it was very difficult to *return* from Palestine to Germany, one had to turn one's heart inside out redo the whole route in the opposite direction, which now in this direction is abrupt, and carpeted with sharp stones that cut like knife blades. One drags oneself bleeding in the blood's reverse direction [*en sang inverse*], says the text.

—They left for Jerusalem without warning? I asked.
—Without warning her, says the tragedy. They wanted to surprise her, they said.

They were exalted. They were trembling. They had sold off everything before leaving. The beautiful house on Friedrichstrasse. The automobile too. Except for the factory, which was co-owned. Here is Andreas on the way there beneath his travel rug and his bag full of books. Here is Andreas, on the return trip, like an actor terrorized by the necessity of improvising he looks for two words to say, he can't find them, he is now nothing but a ghost who would like to end it. It's the ghost who told Rosi the story of the hellish night. He found nothing to say. Next to the enormity of his pain, that night of general inhumanity was not a big deal.

—Break! Shatter! Burn! You are killing only walls and store windows. My heart can no longer be devoured. I left it to rot in Palestine. Impaled!

—In act II the daughter sends the father away, says the tragedy. One cannot imagine a more unbearable scene in the life of an aging father. Pity has not even ever been born. Yet as in a Shakespeare play, after the worst there strikes worse than the worst: while the father returns crawling into the German dungeon falls act III: Irmgard's supreme cruelty: to die behind his back! The old man crawls. The tragedy drives a nail into his eye. Zuckerkrönchen dead! There is nothing left to desire but the grave. Worse, better: to go to the Jerusalem of the unfortunate, take the Dust train to reach the Dust terminus and there finally be dispersed.

—I do not hide from you, says the book, the secret trait of Andreas's destiny is not that he was returned to the murderers by his own daughter, at least apparently, it's that during the last years of wandering in Osnabrück itself, in the hurricanes, the mad vagabond had only one hope: to find the address of his death.

He is looking for the address of his death
The Nazis merely realized his most secret wish: they suicided him.

Just and unjust, I am dead, I want to forget myself, I want not to be and never to have been.
You will look for me in the dust and I will no longer be there

—There is a tragedy hidden in the Tragedy that no one has the strength to talk about. It's a midget tragedy woven of sins and innocences in which all the characters have reasons to reproach all the characters, rage blows, at the idea of god, at the idea of love, reasons for reproach, there is no forgiveness, only griefs and cruel surprises. That there is a tragedy hidden in a blackened fold of the Tragedy, that is what's tragic. If I didn't write, says the book, no one would know anything about the true Passion of Andreas

Everyone would bury him under the rubble of memory.

Omi was under a parasol at Paradise beach.

She was afraid of getting a sunburn.

—The candidate for death Jonas Andreas was declared successively at Goethestrasse 27, Gutenbergstrasse 5, Nikolai-ort 2, Friedrichstrasse 25, Grossestrasse 44, he was looking for the end, in vain his bones pierced his soul, it drags on, it drags on, who will give me death? says the book.

—*Declared*, what does that mean? I say.

—It means something frightening like a sickness of the language, a plague that spread throughout the city, words that before were familiar and inoffensive swelled into buboes, they ceased to ruminate, they came to have teeth curved like claws, they turned against their users the way rabid dogs attack their masters, they ran through the streets growling, especially words in *-ung*, those words that had been known *before* as active, deserving citizens, they spread their frightful growlings, no one recognized them any more, as soon as one heard them *-ung -ung -ung* one was seized by a death anguish, one knew that they were going to unleash, in the inoculated language they had scorpioned, commands that were totally incomprehensible but whose indication was always the same whatever may have been the prescription and it was: judeoextirpation

-dung, -tung (pronounced *oung*, guttural, like *ang*, in anguish, unguish, ounguish), *-bung, -rung*

who among us, when we were learning the beautiful German language in school, could have imagined that this friendly and honorable suffix *-ung*, whose vocation consists in transforming a verb into a noun, a devoted agent, the little genius of the desire to act, to continue, to pursue, all of which is most desirable, then, would become, in the years of fire, the worrisome auxiliary of all the persecutorial inventions. Vertreibung. Vernichtung. Entrechtung.

-ung!
the sound of the knell for all the inhabitants on whose faces Authority had imprinted the mark *Jude*, an imprint whose action was the instant metamorphosis of people into cattle, that is to say, youdification.

All of a sudden every youdified individual was ordered to / condemned to a double allocation / sanction / punishment / obligation: to be submitted to a double injunction-obligation-sanction: with every movement-displacement in space, the registered one must on the one hand be declared (announced, signaled, proclaimed) on the other signal himself, present himself at the police station in every street, himself record his declaration of presence on the street, do his act of denunciation by the rules, precede himself, follow himself, escort himself, confess himself, *sich melden*, with each delocalization, relocalization proceed with the updating of his trace by Abmeldung, Unmeldung, Meldung, regularize each uprooting, expulsion, crossing off, cancellation, expectoration, thus watch over being watched over, exist only with the existence controlled by a passbook of existence

on the model of the management of the leper-always-preceded-by the tinkling of the leper's bell

IT IS RIGHT AROUND THIS MOMENT THAT ÈVE KLEIN, WHO WILL SOON BE MY MOTHER, first presented herself to the Dresden police station, in order to declare that she was coming from Paris, France, where she would return in eight days after having visited her mother Rosalie Jonas Widow Klein — presently lodging with her sister Hete Jonas, her brother-in-law is director of the Dresdnerbank — so as to obtain a visitor's permit, before being able to meet her mother, it was really the last of the last times, the one that marked the last passport of my mother with an indelible visa. Because for eternity she was *declared* exited from Germany by the port of Dresden, *signaled exitedJewess*.

How do you expect me to tell you what I felt, I don't remember, I have other things to think about, you just have to imagine, says my mother, because of this visit to Omi later I was *declared* last domiciled in Dresden, East Germany.

—Maman! Did you say Heil Hitler in the visa bureau? I forgot to ask you this question. I don't know how to imagine this scene. Answer me in a dream.

—I know one thing: already in 1933 my cousin Kurt Löwenstein was arrested in Osnabrück because he was taking photos of posters plastered on a Jewish store. *Achtung! Juden!*

But a post card is enough,
     it was sent from Theresienstadt to Osnabrück, it bears a stamp of the Deutsches Reich, Hitler's left profile in effigy, valid for all countries in the Reich, Bohemia, Moravia, Czechoslovakia. On the bottom left of the card, you read
     Der Führer kennt nur Kampf,
     Arbeit und Sorge.
     Wir wollen Ihm den Teil abnehmen
     Den wir ihm abnehmen können

so that you can begin to imagine

And do you know this word: *Entjudung?* Dejudification. Disinjudification
     O sweet German language, supple friend of the poets, you were treated like a concentration camp judeoguineapig, on your tender cat's body were grafted crocodile fragments, fangs were implanted in your words
     In Oran, when, designated by fate to fulfill the function of spokesperson for the dead, Omi began to play her part, I didn't notice that there were these silences. I didn't know that I didn't know. I didn't hound my grandmother. I didn't unearth the dead. When I wanted to interrogate my mother, I gave up: her stories didn't remember the previous stories

Leaving Marga

—You should perhaps question Marga, the book suggests to me.

I was not convinced. It would be an unexpected turn. Marga? After the disappearance of all the witnesses and contemporaries, more than seventy years having crumbled on the stage, there is no longer anyone to say: I knew the Jonas family, they knew the Engers, the Engers knew the van Pels, the van Pels knew the Franks, Peter van Pels rode his bike with Horst, Horst stole Ève's (my mother's) bike, which she had borrowed from or lent to Grete Bloch, the daughter of the veterinarian, Felix Nussbaum I knew him my mother said, this memory was perhaps created by her when she was more than a hundred years old, before that it had never come to mind, one can't say that Ève knew/did not know Felix Nussbaum

Leaving Marga?

In the end, one was looking at the map of the Zentrum of Osnabrück, and one no longer knew who had known had not known whom, everyone knew, one had known whom one hadn't known, everyone passed by, had strolled, had entered, had bought, had seen, had spoken, had learned, had swum, had made an excursion to the forest, had passed the Abitur, had eaten, had had secrets, was dead.

Leaving Marga.

Marga, what's left of Ève.

The first time Marga telephoned me, it was the day that I had had to let my mother depart. For a moment I thought I was hearing the voice of Éri, my mother's sister. But that isn't possible. She's been dead for ten years. Yet it is that voice. Their voice. Then I thought I heard the echo of Ève's voice. It was that somewhat crumpled, somewhat bitten English captured by the German timbre. Because it's a day of revenants, I thought. Hallucinating, I staggered between "death" and the flight into life. I said —Marga? Then she said: Hélène! Now we had not heard each other's voices for

decades. I didn't even know that Marga was not like Ève
and Éri, dead, dead. — It's Marga and she's alive! I say to my
daughter. Moreover she was speaking — whereas my mother
was "lips sealed," that's what she slipped to me in silence.

— She's doing her self-portrait, I say to my daughter.

I was seized by wonder. She was all-powerful. — She plays
Scrabble, I say. And cooking? She cooks. I thought I saw
my mother standing on her one hundred years. But today
for the first time she was lying down. I admired Marga, I
had a moment of felicity, after all Marga is cut from the
same cloth as Maman. Then I had a rush of jealousy. She
is not suffering from anything. She has all her wits? Just like
my mother. — Like haute couture, says my mother. She was
looking for the rhyme. Finally she found it: ich bin am Tür.
I laughed till I cried.

She was in Jerusalem.

Marga is still alive. Having passed her 105th year, she is now
the only one to have power still over the disappeared do-
main, she alone can help me. All the characters in our books
are below ground. One might think she's approaching silence, but not at all. Certainly one can telephone her. I have
her number in Jerusalem. Finally her path led her to Jerusalem. At the beginning she left from Gemen near Osnabrück where she often goes to visit family, Ève often goes to
Gemen, they have a sister-life by cousinage, the same, she
too leaves Germany at the right moment, she too goes to
Strasbourg, then she turns up in Ireland, from there to England in London. She lives in Golders Gardens in Golders
Green, that's where I meet her, I'm thirteen years old, my
mother sends me from Algeria to the English Golden Garden. I loved Marga in English

But I will not go to Jerusalem to see her. If I do go, it will
be to give in to an order come from my highest internal

antiquity. I will go alone, without ancestor, without love, without descendent. No one will be waiting for me, I will be waiting for myself only at the end. I don't know yet if I will manage to go there in this book.

—I find it bizarre that she never called *before*, says the book. What's the point of calling *after*, when Ève has just left? If she had called a few days earlier . . . I will not tell you what I think, says the book.

To conclude I promise that I will call her for her birthday now that I have her number. And I will do it, I promise myself. Marga began like Ève with two children. But from there came thirteen grandchildren and perhaps sixteen. And from there fifty great-grandchildren, according to the *Jerusalem Post*. As if all by herself she would raise all the dead, she would go from the family to the village to the whole city. There is no explanation. Chance rules. Chance rules everything and the rest.

And the husband?

—One can't tell everything, I say. —If I had the time, says the book, I could. —One cannot tell the truth, I say, no book, I cannot, no one will ever be able to tell the truth, and that's too bad. And it's fortunate. Instead of that Illusion one can say everything and it will be invented truth.

Since this telephone call Marga and Co. have been augmented by three great-grandchildren. She is able to say their names, but it's possible she invents them

And yet she exists, and she lives, in reality, in Jerusalem.

It's incomprehensible

No one will ever understand God, says the Book of Job. I don't know if it's a matter of understanding. No one will ever understand Job. The sorrows, all of literature barely suffices to evoke them. And he is left deprived of death, he has life only so as to have no end of suffering. You recall that all the apples of his eye are torn from him at one blow, all his children, all his children, not even the tiniest infant is left to him, he's left with only the word *infant* like a flaming stake in his eye, I say to my daughter.

When in the thirtieth chapter no one any longer has the strength to follow me, says the book, God decides to speak to him, God himself has dined on horror and boredom. He's had enough of hearing Job's friends speak in his defense, saying God knows what he's doing, you have sinned, God would not swoop down on you if you weren't guilty, and to hear Job shout I am innocent, God knows what he's doing, and me I know that I did nothing.

So He says: —Insect, how could you understand me or

imagine me? For a dog I have Leviathan. Do you have any idea what I had to do to Kreate a Kreature so terrifyingly perfect? To say nothing of the millions of monsters and unknown species.

And Job says, honest: —That is true, I understand nothing at all. I am innocent, that is true. On the other hand, there are monstrous sorrows. Where is the logic? It's all the same to me. God, that's all. In my language, the Job language, that phrase is equivocal. Understand it with Your language.

And so He says: —I see you have understood me. You understand nothing, and so you understand. But the others, your friends, leave them out of it.

I will thus be incomprehensible like God, says He: in a first moment I ripped everything away from you. In the last part I am going to shower you with all the riches, herds, buildings. Note that there is *no* relation between the two parts of your destiny. No consequence. No punctuation. You will have seven sons and three daughters . . . So Job has ten children. He is content with his new children.

—I don't understand him, I say to my daughter.

He doesn't look back. He doesn't complain about having lost his former children. He leaves the pain in the forty parts where it exploded. In the last part he takes pleasure right up to his last day. I'm speaking of Job.

—It's magnificent, says my daughter.

—It's terrible, I say.

—He doesn't give in, says my daughter, He doesn't replace.

—I don't understand. I don't understand He. I don't understand why so many hundreds of creatures, brothers, sisters, cousins, friends from long ago, parents, mortals, hunted, dispossessed, killed, separated, why Marga, the little sister of Kürt Löwenstein, and the twin cousin of my mother, lives after the limit, and she sees that more and more children are added to the sixty-five all of whose names she doesn't manage to retain.

Is it a blessing to have so many children who have so many children who have so many children that one ends up being less and less sensitive to death? At the fourth generation death does not last, is not hard.

If Marga is the daughter of aunt Paula, one of Rosi's sisters
    One of the nondeported, unless she was deported
    Then surviving
    From Paula to today a crowd descends.
    From Andreas the older brother of Rosi and Paula
    Who descends? Are there descendants?

Should I ask Inès of Chile? Would Inès of Chile be the ultimate peripeteia of the story? Inès had fled Chile and taken refuge in Paris at my mother's home, repeating in 1973 my mother's escape in 1929 then 1933, for the story begins again on another shore, Satan reprises his devastation, the evil is the same only the language changes, and this whole plot was in Spanish. Was Inès the continuation of Hans Günther Jonas? Was the latter the son of Andreas Jonas? Memories are lacking.

One speaks little of King Lear's son. All the tragic tension is fed by the daughter. The son will forever remain withdrawn in a distant obscurity. This character figures in the notes. I don't know if this is the book's choice or my mother's. What troubles me is this obscurity. What gives me pause is the presence of homonyms. Several Hans Gunthers rise up in memory to the call of this name, one in South Africa, the other in Chile, there was one in Australia, but his trace was lost.

Inès of Chile exists. When she arrived in Paris she spoke not a word of French. If I had her telephone number, I would ask her: —Inès, a ghost, the ghost of old Andreas, the decrowned of Osnabrück, does he haunt your memory? Is there one of these old men who resemble the painful grotesques that come to us from Germany in the tales of Hoffmann, in your dreams? An old man who talks to himself in a low voice, dressed in misery, but whose face under the grime still has a curiously modern and familiar aspect? And who would be your grandfather?

But I no longer have Inès's address, she no longer has her German name in Chilean, the last time, having married at a turn of the story's thread a French electrician, she traveled in memories under the name of Inès B. That is a name that led me nowhere in the vast genealogical library — whose curator I have just learned from a dream is an archivist named Spinoza — a series of tiled, windowless rooms where are disseminated incomplete documents vestiges of the myriads of characters who came from the primitive tree of Osnabrück, in an irresponsible jumble.

My mother mentioned two thousand of them. I was loath to shelter so many dead and so many opinions. Concerning the political points of view, I am almost certain that I would have found myself in disagreement with most of the tenants of our memory.

I do not imagine

I LEFT FOR OSNABRÜCK FROM THE NORTH STATION, AND NOT THE EAST STATION, as I had written that my mother dreamed of doing. In *Osnabrück*, the book that has the same name as the city, the character who has the same name as my mother has but one desire: "to go to Osnabrück, Osnabrück, Osnabrück" the exact contrary of my mother's desire in reality, moreover she would never have said Osnabrück Osnabrück Osnabrück that was not her style, this repetition, it's a coquetry of the book that speaks French, a way of titillating the ear of the French-speaking reader, Osnabrück in French is untranslatable into German, the rough and abrupt charm of its syllables is nothing, for the German Osnabrück is a hamster, in the language of the book it's a hedgehog. My mother thinks it's not interesting to overdo it, people are already sufficiently hostile to this German language

I left from French to go to German in the same city, in the same breath, and in truth, I went there as one goes to Jerusalem, the city where one spends one's life promising, to which one dreams that one will end up by (not having been there) having been there only too late, after the life of promise, the way Proust cannot go to Venice without all the detours of the French language, he barely avoids the venom of the wordplay, the way Freud who has tears only for Rome finds himself transferring his passions and his resistances onto *the other eternal city*

I went there like the nostalgia for Ithaca long after the Odyssey when no one is left alive, and like the triumph of the future when on the amnesiac ground where even the ruins have been expelled, one leans down and says: rise up. What remained of Osnabrück for my mother were the tales, she had given them to me over and over, they were countless short narratives, lives with German first names, images of living rooms and kitchens, sounds of clocks, the superanimated décor of her schoolgirl world, a crowd, characters called Hilde, Hans, Gerta, Selma, Kurt, Max, Hans-Günther, Siegfried, Fred, Herbert, Otto, Hete, the names fluttered about and alighted now on one destiny, now on another, there were also several Moritzes, Hanses, Horsts, Jennys, the little Selma and the big Selma, the one who was very rich and the one who was not, the miser, the gambler, the debtor, the wise man, the jokester, the poet, the entrepreneur, in the end the whole Commedia of Osnabrück had been blown away by the Great Explosion and dispersed in splinters and pieces of passport pages over the continents, and the tales whirled round, inebriated by planetary distances. But the city whose all-powerful delirium had notified her with Entrechtung, Vertreibung, Hasse, Qual, Schrei und Schreck, no, she could not say its name, and its first name was *Not*.

Like cats that interiorize instantly a message of danger likewise my mother is always on alert, her suitcase ready. How
frail is trust and how perpetual mistrust!

The two sisters Ève and Éri are united, they are wary of me,
there is someone, they sense, who suffers from a lack of mistrust, that girl is traumatized by phantasm, she is not the
bearer of spiritual scarifications, she can look with a biol-
ogist's curiosity at the signs tacked to the chest of shattered
buildings in the streets of November '38 she takes up a mag-
nifying glass to examine the samples of howling texts,
    she *examines* what makes us vomit and pour sweat
    we will not go
    they say, embarrassed,
    to be sure the delirium
    has disappeared
    however those edicts still burn that ordered us
    to leave the earth and camp at the edge of humanity
    the people are very nice, they received us very well

Liebste Helene

Nach guter Reiser kamen wir in einem netten Hotel. Wir spazierten durch schöne Strassen mit alten Prunkhäusern lauter Kaufhäusern. Leider ist es kalt: Eben kommen wir aus einem gemütlichen Restaurant wo gut und zu viel assen. Morgen ist ein busy day with the mayor, a woman. Love and kisses, your loving mother

Gruss aus Osnabrück

—Is it the first time, the first time you come to Osna-brück? the Oberbürgermeister asks me. He is shiny very big very, his uniform is decorated with embroideries and gold braids, and he bends his young innocent head over me exactly like that tulip tree flowering in front of the entrance to the Rathaus bends over the visitor, while tracing a graceful curve. Ist es das erste Mal? the mayor asks me. And I too ask myself the question. Is it the first time? It is not the first time that I ask myself this question. But, it seems to me, it is the first time that the question is presented to me by such a charming and richly colored actor, to the point that when he entered, the whole scene became mythological, and thus I was assured that this time we found ourselves in a city of literature. Everything was metaphor and metonymy. Invention and quotation.

But never have I seen such a springtime, at least one so like a dream of springtime, the trees rebel with the airs of Proustian young girls, ravishing my attention, it is the first time that April seems to me so seductive, I feel I am in Ovid,

I sense that I find myself on metamorphosis street, such a juvenile décor promises festivals and weddings.

It is not the first time I have been asked this question, I mused, yet it is the first time that I discern, beneath the gewöhnlich aspect of these words, extraordinary powers of philosophical, cinematographic, historical evocation. One says these words and whole Cities rise up, what am I saying, they are: The Cities. O seasons of celebrations and promises of ruins! Osnabrück, first name of Jerusalem and Calcutta, of Babylon, canticle of quanticles, root and cradle of the Tristias of all my childhoods, those of my mothers and my unknown grandmothers

I owe an answer to this mayor among all the mayors, this time it's a dream in which I am not dreaming

—Is it the first time, that you, to Osnabrück come?

And coming from all of Europe that day forty-eight sovereigns crowd into the Great Hall of the Rathaus, which, in reality, is very small, so that once seated on the benches that circle the room, they are so huddled against one another that they form, in an unexpected feature of this so very famous occasion, something like a single royal nest. All have their faces turned toward the Supermayor and me, four hundred years stand at the windows, photos are taken. The Supermayor makes a well-crafted little speech, he is extremely tall, nothing has changed, except the size of the men of our time, I regret that Maman is not here, this regret threatens to cut off my speech, but if my mother were here, she would have found all this useless, too late.

—You don't know the treaty of Westphalia? I say. —That doesn't interest me, History, she says; it's just a war. I prefer geography. If you take Osnabrück by events, it's without me.

But for my misfortune my mother is not there and it's I who am there, in Osnabrück, as if I couldn't prevent myself from being the imposture. As if I had been obliged to come to Osnabrück, in spite of her and in spite of it, in spite of my mother, in spite of me, in spite of Osnabrück.

. . . das erste Mal? says the voice of the great Tulip Tree.

I ask myself, this time rigorously, as if it were the first and the last. *Weder oder nicht*, one good time.

But I don't know if it is the first time. I have perhaps already come to Osnabrück, I don't know if I didn't go to Osnabrück with Omi as I believe that I went, the first time that I went to Germany with Omi I was fourteen years old, the first time that Omi "came back" to Germany we went to Köln, for a good and lamentable reason about which I will say nothing in this book, we went to the Cathedral, where we probably really did not wish to go, but all the same we did it, my grandmother said nothing, we ate a pineapple tart called Domtorte, the cathedral Tart eaten, my grandmother thought, from there we perhaps went to Osnabrück there are two trains a day, I don't see a train, I am not sure. I see a tram in a narrow street of Osnabrück, but is it from memory or is it a constructed memory?

But the mayor is a tall, handsome, innocent man, a shining Tulip Tree. I would like to please him. Give him the answer. But I have no proofs of truth. When I began to worry, suddenly I asked myself about the nature of my images of Osnabrück, are these memories different in substance from phantasms, dreams, they are trembling, intense, dog-eared, fragmented, moving, did I go, Omi had just left. Or else: when Omi left, I woke up with a start, as if I were running to the station carried by the fear of missing the train, I wanted to ask her, "Omi! Wait! Did we go are we going to Osnabrück?" but she was already far away. I remember, I telephoned Éri, who now was no longer in Palestine, that is to say Israel, was no longer in Köln, but was in Manchester, did I go to Osnabrück from Köln? do you remember? But in vain. In Manchester all of that was the past. My other-memory was forlorn, had become pale, begun to turn yellow like a leaf, started to quake like an adieu, to resemble one of those photos of the Jonas building on *Nikolaiort* taken by the photographer Lichtenberg and that trouble us when we see them preserved in the catalogues of the city: the older the views of the house, the more the house looks young and strong.

And so, I exclaimed: Yes! Herr Oberbürgermeister!

Of course it is the first time in a certain way, the first posthumous time, alone, so withoutmaman

and this love that I have, that I would never have had in front of Maman, that my mother will never have had, for Jerusalem-Osnabrück

As if Maman had become Osnabrück, that's how I go there, as if she were waiting for me, as if I expected to see her come toward me at the corner of the Great Street, as if I were going to be able to cry out Maman! I would listen to the notes of the cry in French in the German air and she would quicken her pace which was always rapid toward me while smiling at me, and now I see her she is showing me her German purchase, *ein Knirps* naturally, it is only here that one makes such practical umbrellas

as if I was going there so as to cry out come back! and not only does she come back, and to find her again alive, because in Osnabrück she is never dead, almost all are dead, but she, she always knew where life was, and in good health, and escorted by a group of words that I had totally forgotten and that are just waiting for an occasion, she dashes at a surprising regular speed and as if standing still, like the duck surrounded by her numerous ducklings supernaturally rapid dashes, they dash, on the lustrous bronze silk of the Hase

—BUT WHAT HAVE I COME HERE TO DO?

At dawn, I make the rounds of the city, before the inhabitants are up, I am looking for what I am looking for, I go around the Dom with my mother remembered, we pass in front of the Carolinum, the little school founded by Karl der Grosse,

—You said nothing to me, my young Ève with long braids, about the lamentable history of 2 Nikolaiort, the word *Ariesirung*, you didn't pronounce it. We were walking quickly on the paving stones of the deserted spruced-up Zentrum.

I swear I didn't know the date of Kristallnacht, that broken night that for me was but one night among all the dishonored nights of the century, our dawn is tepid and soft like a dream of humanity, the sky is made of tulip tree petals before the entrance of color, we are looking for the Hase, not History, geography

and we don't find it, would it be expelled from the city, repressed, buried? your river eliminated. I interrogate the Supermayor, what have I come to look for?

my beloved, where are you?

The Guest Book is gigantic, how everything is bigger than big *here!* The Supermayor, the Book, Memory,

yet how skeleton-like, amnesiac I am, my tongue is hampered, my sentences stutter in German

the Supermayor shows me the signatories my predecessors are kings of all the countries, ministers, imposters, provisionals, heroes, rhetors, the whole sovereign world, among which I am going to be introduced, they look for Günter Grass, in vain, that worries-reassures me that one can escape from the enclosure of the Guest Book, *here* —sign—

Have I come to sign?

I am surrounded by legitimate international dictators and executioners

and how small and gloriously modest and modestly proud the hall of the Rathaus is

enormous, the heart of the City of Peace is a fat book that weighs a hundred pounds

—*Here,* says the Supermayor, Atlas today carries centuries that hatred and peace have fought over without bending his spine.

Ève, Éri, Omi, Onkel André, the Engers cast equivocal looks at me — "what are *we* doing here?" say the eyes and the looks seek where to light, where to hide, but the walls are covered with faces that are dressed in royal compunction before the lens of Time. But the fact that among so many gentlemen there is the half-smile of Christine of Sweden and the warm gaze of the Bürgermeisterin Karin Jabs-Kiesler comes to my aid. We are no longer in the butcher shop called *The Twentieth Century.* In our play, the word "feminist" is as common as the "@" and when I sign, my mother signs next to my signature, I note that she draws her German maiden name, and next comes the signature of Rosi Klein. That's

Omi, my grandmother, I say to Atlas, and his eyes twinkle
with humidity, for he too has, he says, an Omi in his heart.

Between my two hands I have trouble holding the
memory-work of the City, a gray cement block from which
a little knight cut out in metal tries to drag his horse, the
figurine rears up in the direction of Münster, the sister-city
of Osnabrück where, in the twin Rathaus, the other kings
heads of state cardinals and tyrants are waiting to counter-
sign the treaty that puts an end to the massacres four hundred years before the beginning of the end of the massacres.
I signed only half the peace, I say to myself. How heavy is
the honorific block of Osnabrück. It's because you cannot
imagine how much peace weighs when it tries to escape the
grave. Abmeldung nach Zukunft

It looks like Titan's large die, and on its four sides an
anonymous artist has handwritten in black on gray Recht
Friede Toleranz Wissen. That is to say Peace Tolerance
Knowledge Law that is to say Tolerance Knowledge Right
Peace

But what am I doing here?
So late

It is very difficult to make the truth of this journey because it
keeps on growing, exceeding me, refuting me, abusing me
and disabusing me
　　—What have you come to do *here*?
　　—I have come to cultivate ruin and flourish memory

While I am going back up Krahnstrasse, then Herrenstrasse
to Schillerstrasse, raising my eyes to caress distractedly with
my gaze the tops of the houses that are not very high and
carefully maintained, for at ten o'clock on this morning a
cool and blue light bathes a still unoccupied neighborhood,

there is no traffic, people are sleeping, a timelessness of dream extends its last instants before the entrance of the inhabitants onto their daily stage,

and I too walk without noise so as not to waken the sleeping families as if I was sleeping myself,

I do not know that a gathering of 30,000 persons that is to say at least one person per family, the city having on that day 95,000 inhabitants, is vociferating in unison the demand to purge the city by elimination of those Jews agents of ruin and contamination, they total two hundred and thirty in the last town census. This unitary demonstration is so massive that it would crack the edges of the streets if it were not so rigorously surrounded and ordered beneath its supple walls of high-flying banners of the Reich, in this beautiful springtime of 1935

—It doesn't bother you to be honored by Osnabrück on April 20? Anna raises the leaden question in such a delicate way that I don't feel the weight, I think it's a paper question. But I don't know that Hitler was born one April 20 and on April 20, 2015, it had never been a fairer day in Osnabrück it was like an Oran day and the springtime was congratulating itself for having decked out the city just in time.

While passing in Krahnstrasse I notice with the tip of my right foot a paving stone that is different from the indigenous paving stones, a foreign element like the gold tooth in Felice Bauer's jaw. An ambiguous jewel, a hole turned into a gilded bridle bit. I have just the time to lengthen my step slightly. In the sweet distraction in which the sugary air immerses me I was about to step on the face of an aurified deceased one. I stare at the little paving stone, it turns out it is a talking stone, as in one of my dreams, it says to me I am a book, I am here not to make you stumble but to make you open your eyes. Do you know where you are putting your feet? I was made for you, the passersby, who come after me. I too used to pass by Krahnstrasse, planets were struck down gulfs opened up, gangs of demons settled into the neighborhoods of Osnabrück but I am tired of repeating my story and you who are living after my epic, you chew gum and don't listen to me, is this going to last a long time this threnody? you think, no, no, yes, yes, I hear you, so I stop and I sum up my Iliad in eleven words, and, philosopher, I have but two words to say to you: *Remember me.*

Whoever you may be, says the talking stone, and whoever I may be, I am still the ghost of the ghost of your father. All of us, a people melted down and poured out, young, old, women, men, fathers, daughters and sons, we are a single orphan adopted by memory our mother.

This five-inch square book says to mine: as for me, I am the book that you don't have the strength to write, I am the done book. You are the world, I am the temple.

The Stolpersteine in Herder Strasse, or Martinistrasse, are they beings or paving stones? Or animated stones? Do they suffer? When passing by Katharinenstrasse does one avoid putting one's foot on the face of the letters? What does the sole think of it?

The one hundred ninety-two Jewish paving stones of Osnabrück are polished. According to me the two hundred sixty-seven bronze stones are polished by politeness. But perhaps they were polished by the rubbing of the millstones of the Philistines who observed the agony of Samson.

Dear memory stones, uncles, aunts, mummified parents, masks of the sacrificed, I send you greetings from Osnabrück,

Nach guter Reise kam ich in einem netten Haus an und fand Ève, Omi, Éri und Gruppe, lauter netten Frauen von heute vor. Wir spazierten durch rauschende sprechende Strassen. I had the surprise of finding a team of very committed archangels, I know it is not a consolation for those of you who passed through the slaughterhouse, but for me who reads the newspapers of today while exhaling a *world, world, o world* of disgust, it was a plea in defense of humanity. These ministers and mayoresses on the left wing of the party like Gabriel, Michael and Co., being virgins of despair, I didn't say a word of what I was thinking

—I think they look Jewish, whispers Éri. —Nonsense, murmurs my mother. It's she, Éri, my mother's little sister, who has the role of the child in *The Emperor's New Clothes*. She is always playing tricks on Truth, as a dressmaker, she knows a lot about veils and cottons.

If someone is going to eat a pork chop in the cafeteria of the Rockefeller Building where she's been invited by Richard Katz, the most humbly orthodox of the cousins, it's that Éri, says my mother.

Warm, enthusiastic women, who delight in books like they're whipped cream, bearing their middle age with charm and eagerness, the feminist Bürgermeisterin, the militant woman director of the Erich Maria Remarque-Friedens-Zentrum, barely have we been introduced ten minutes earlier than it's done and we've known each other since forever and we can lend each other husbands if we have them like Frau Engers to Rosi. Women of Osnabrück, excuse me, I am merely transcribing the feeling of known-since-forever that Freud talks about, which has just made an impression on my aunt Éri.

—I don't know where we're going, says my mother. —25 Friedrichstrasse, I say to the taxi driver. And what if I hadn't found the address of the ghost of Andreas Jonas on the internet? —I am going to visit the totally abandoned ghost of a miserable character who resembles the wreck without desire and without defense of Colonel Chabert, the living posthumous one, I say.

The taxi climbs toward the heights of West Osnabrück,

passes by the château, turns onto Westerberg hill, no one
ever told me there was another Osnabrück, now the houses
throw out their chests, line up their baroque decorations,
now they lower an eyebrow as I pass by, no one ever told me
about the well-to-do hill the sumptuous façades, I never visited an uncle in Neuilly, a state of alert to the *Unheimliche*
takes hold of me on Uhlandstrasse, how far we are, it seems
to me that my boat has been carried very far from the port
of Nikolaiort, there's been an error, there's been some er-
rancy, the taxi driver has changed, at the corner of Bismarck-
strasse he has donned a uniform, where are we going, we
continue going up, here we are in the land of grand houses,
the annual incomes exceed now my imagination, at heights
that my sight fails to measure, Olympian and exuding the
strange serenity of the very rich, stand Proustian allusions to
the Upper East Side, and I don't dare ask the driver if he has
made a mistake, I am not well enough dressed. It's as if while
believing one is going the way of Méséglise I found myself
accidentally on the way of Guermantes, and my sneakers
leave me no chance of deserving a visa. But, although I
murmur, the car leaves me in front of 25 Friedrichstrasse,
whose entrance painted gold has an elegance far beyond
my middle-class calculations. Three more steps and there
would be as valet a chambermaid, someone from the country who is making her way and who had hoped the son of
the household would not find her displeasing, but this novel
breaks down one summer day in 1935, over the laws of purity
of German blood and can go no further than this phantasm
made forever outmoded by the Nazi superforce. Since September 15 the date on which it's not just that a Jude/Jew can
no longer be a civil servant, as is the case since the *Arierpara-
graph* of April 11, 1933, it's not just that all of Germany, the
whole Reich, that is to say the whole party is called upon to
define in a totally precise manner what being a Jew is, what
is Jew, what is being, what is: being, what being is, pure is

always perhaps already probably not altogether purely pure, who knows who slept with whom, who had perhaps hidden flat feet or a nose perhaps a little less straight than straight and thus perhaps a tad youdific

how to realize the will the swill of Hitler to separate the Jude thing from the body of the nation, the *Schmarotzer*, how to delouse oneself, deyoudify oneself, deblemish oneself, how to protect the superblood of the German people from the risk of contact with a contaminating loathsome subblood

but it's that Jews are forbidden to have household employees of German blood younger than forty-five so as to exclude any risk of Rassenverrat, a betrayal of the race punishable by the death penalty

The chambermaid intercepts me and has me wait in the salon, no doubt there's a concert or a bridge game that must not be disturbed, and while I look at the silver looking at me looking at it, my brain recites its sociology but very poorly: "bourgeois, aristocrat, affluent, fortune, and income," I have only abstract and lifeless tools, meanwhile the decoration of the grand house compels admiration whether I like it or not, for I have never seen such a refined interior in my life. "Siren!" I exclaim. And as I return with a backward jump onto the welcoming sidewalk, the hallucination melts away like ghosts at dawn.

I had not been warned. An immense powerless and pitifully anachronic pity leaps to the rescue of Onkel André and in vain, but what are you doing there, oh unhappy one! it cries, you found nothing better than to settle in the neighborhood where gold is naturally allied with your death? Blackbird, you made your nest in the home of buzzards? Get out of there! Don't you see your bed is burning?

It stares you in the face

It will be two hundred years, since Balzac, that we've known, the neighborhoods of cities play in our destinies the role of the gods who work for or against us in the *Odyssey*. I

have never been to Neuilly, but Wikipedia would warn any candidate looking for a lodging of the ethical and political consequences that accompany the apartment. My mother says nothing. But it stares you in the face, I say, that we are visiting a neighborhood where the top people in the party assured the cohesion of the group. It's a nest, don't you see that it's a nest? I'm not saying my mother denies. But she prefers to say nothing.

But in vain pity sounds the alarm: mad and a beggar the old man falters and his eyes are as if he were blind, he wants to see only his pelican daughter.

Friedrich Street is sleeping. Westerberg rises late. And on the sidewalk in front of 25, two Stolpersteine defy me with their bronze eyes that never close.

Here lies the Andreas Jonas dossier recorded in the archive of Eternity. "Here lived Andreas Jonas to be deported and killed 09/06/1942"

Andreas JONAS
geboren am 05.02.1869 in Borken
STRASSE: Friedrichstrasse 25
STADTTEIL: Westerberg
TODESDATUM: 06.06.1942
TODESORT: Theresienstadt

Else JONAS, geb. Cohn
geboren am 09.07.1880 in Rostock
STRASSE: Friedrichstrasse 25
STADTTEIL: Westerberg
TODESDATUM: 25.01.1944
TODESORT: Theresienstadt

We, the biographical paving stones, we are the whole truth of Jonas Andreas

I scrutinize the street of truth, it descends from 25 down

to the heart of the city of Osnabrück, it is a young woman, stylish and slender, bordered with flowering trees, o family, I thought, family, how silent you are how you spread over your loved ones the tender and amoral protection of secrecy! How you hide the pain beneath silk!

—Onkel André was rich! —What difference does that make? —It adds a bitter note to the tragedy. —If you say so. When I listened to my mother recount the tale I never thought: a family of eight children, some prosper. Some are in difficulty, like Omi my grandmother. A war widow, no profession, no savings. Some very rich. The poor don't imagine that the rich are rich. In the end all of them come together equal in mud and in dust. My friend Anna looks at the two little bronze masks. She says: now I understand that Andreas was able to help his little sister your grandmother. Then I will say: but he never helped his little sister! A golden curtain slightly raised. The more fortunate brothers and sisters, what did they do for Rosi the youngest sister? Except Uncle Moritz from South Africa. He comes on purpose from Johannesburg to shake up Uncle Salo from Strasbourg, if you don't pay Rosi a small pension, I'll punch your lights out, and it was done, says my mother. But I can say nothing here, in Friedrichstrasse. And I add my silence to that of my mother and my grandmother

According to the Jonases, since Michael Klein is the only one of the fourteen Kleins to be killed at the front, and by his own fault on top of everything, since Michael Klein voluntarily joined the German Army, it's up to the other Kleins to guarantee the subsistence of their little sister, that is to say their sister-in-law.

The silence says the truth made by Ève and Omi.

I loved Uncle André very much, says my mother. He didn't dare say no to death

Perhaps I should not have come?

I said that Onkel André was short because on the platform of the Osnabrück station he is the shortest of the four gentlemen who are saying adieu and good-bye, on the station platform, I am so used to seeing him in the stories that I recognize him, he always has a train over his shoulder, that smile that doesn't happen, is he returning, where is he going

and I totally forget to say that the small man in the white shirt is beardless, the idea has never occurred to him to let his beard or mustache grow, whereby he is not so different from his neighbors or mine. Except in his way of listening when the other speaks a little, with seriousness and gentleness. Don't forget to say: I take these indications from The Photo. The Photo is a work of art. It was taken on October 23, 1935. That day it was an act of witnessing on the one hand of friendship on the other of know-how. Later The Photo entered into the world's patrimony. It lives among the visual objects that draw as much from painting as from photography. As a work of art, it passes into an ageless and dateless time, like, at first glance, a portrait of magistrates by Rembrandt.

As for me, I was also seduced by the perfection in space, the play of planes, the interval among the volumes, the power of the characters that occupy the foreground, the work of temporalities that are inscribed in a remarkable condensation, the past growing larger while the future gets lost in the light-shadow of a regret, such that it took me twenty years to break the spell and to recover myself so as to become sensitive again to the message that this splendor obscures. "I am, we are October 23, 1935, do you hear me?" says the message. "It took you a long time!"

I admit it. Not only did it take me a long time, but I had to come to Osnabrück, so late, so late, get off the train at the

Osnabrück station, see the sign on the platform that confirms: *Osnabrück Hauptbahnhof*, see the rails, I was irritated, in 2015, for the date of The Photo of the station to reach my heart finally and regain strength from my life. You see here the last minutes of a century, I'm talking about the Jewish century of Osnabrück, an extraordinarily profound and brief era, which saw the birth, growth, flourishing, and extinction of a human species representative of the life-death cycle of humankind. It is History itself but as it is hidden behind its volumes of commentaries it never sees itself, its image captured in the mirror that catches the eternal essence: the instant of the end where thousands of destinies and events precipitate and are summed up in a single epiphany. The artist gathered up these throbbings. In a few minutes the train will have left, the life of this people of Osnabrück is going to exit the frame forever. *Für immer.* There had to be an artist of the *Fürimmer*, it could only have been Felix Nussbaum, but that day, he was not in Osnabrück, he was perhaps in Ostende or Brussels, so he too is in the photo, en route for the *Fürimmer*. If it's not he then it can only be another Felix.

On the platform of the station where a crowd gathers to which I lend a multitude of feelings and (painful) forebodings Andreas is attentive, no illusion agitates him no anxiety paints a frown on his face

Meanwhile on that day, October 23, 1935, his friend Gustav Stein is leaving Osnabrück *forever*. Meanwhile Andreas Jonas has just returned to Osnabrück forever. Gustav Stein is wearing a cap. The cap of forever. The small man always has his hat. Gustav is leaving at that moment to rejoin his whole family in Palestine. On the photo nothing lets one guess that the heart of the small man on the right is vomiting streams of blood. It's possible moreover that he is not bleeding.

Does one see the forebodings in these photos of the station? One does not see them. That's why I lend the travelers feelings that are too profound to be apparent. If one goes down below the date, to the innermost depths of the soul of the people, there cannot not be a furious commotion of nameless sorrows, of half-muzzled angers, of wounds made by rejected humiliations or accepted humiliations, which never close, of oozing inflammations, of exercises of artificial patience, of duels with oneself and with God, of hand-to-hand combat with discouragement, of training in self-hypnosis and the belief in better worlds in better times in which one doesn't believe, it's a spiritual gymnastics inaugurated in the city already a hundred years ago, only a hundred years ago, founded on the wager of enduring for a duration of, of enduring, that's all, and that hoped to endure for more than a hundred years, all the same more than a long human life, but the train is going to leave in five minutes and the forever of Osnabrück is over. One leaves to look elsewhere for another forever.

The station is the beginning and the end for each of the destinies of the family. In the story the characters come and go with a frequency way above the German average, rise and fall, some even recite their prayers in the train, the train is a country on rails, a brief beyond hope when there is no more hope.

The secret of Osnabrück: it is a railway node unique of its kind. It is the only city in Germany that has at its disposal railway-wise all the cardinal directions. Through Osnabrück pass west-east trains and conversely, as well as north-south trains and conversely. In the other cities there is only one axis. One understands how this double axial potentiality gave rise to, brought about, surreptitiously augmented the mythological vocation of such a city. It is a crossroads, and the only one, for the wanderings and launchings of expeditions of all sorts, exiles, explorations, moves, changes of orientation whether amorous or intellectual or spiritual. One understands that each time Kafka wanted to go to Berlin, he made a detour through Osnabrück. There, while waiting for the connection with another train he could imagine all the consequences in all the directions of a change of mind, he could practice hesitation. From city to city the uncles aunts cousins of my mother were constantly meeting up in a train, driven by the hope of finding in B., a nearby city, a ground and more favorable conditions for a transplant of hope that was dying in G. In the Jonas family one called the station *Hauptbahnhoffnung*. It's a play on words that means Main Station of Hope or Hope at the Main Station.

For a long time I believed that the Jonases were originally from Osnabrück, perhaps even since the thirteenth century. I have checked and the Jonases are indeed originally from my city, but in a dream, as I am in my own way, they seem to have turned around it, staying here and there in Westphalia and in Hanover, and coming closer while moving away over the centuries, tracing on the map the undulation of desire and fear. The last fluctuation will have been produced in truth right before Omi's birth, in the interval between Andreas born still at a little distance from the goal, in Borken, and Rosi born in Osnabrück in 1882. But before her, the *Stationen* book explains to me, it was not possible, Jews did not have the right to be, except by an 1880 law, in Osnabrück. I conclude that as soon as the news was known, Abraham and Helene Jonas took up their places in this history. My relative error comes from the peaceful light that bathes the photo of Helene Meyer sitting at the window of Nikolaiort 2, there emanates from the person of my great-grandmother such an antique and blooming serenity that anyone would have thought she had been installed there for all eternity. It may be that the family had for a generation a certitude of eternity.

To come back to the station platform Andreas is now on the
station platform from which he departed for Jerusalem here
he is departed/returned from Jerusalem, nine months earlier
he was not in the foreground of the photo but in the back-
ground, in the train car precisely there where Frau Stein is
leaning forward slightly to say the good-byes that he was saying he does not look at the train car, he is entirely absorbed
in the contemplation of Gustav Stein's face on which is written: today 10/23/1935 I am leaving *für immer in Palästina*. He
seems, it's probable, to glimpse the reflection of a departed
one. What journeys we make! or rather what a journey! For
finally there is only one and death is the conductor.

How many times, he muses, has he not taken this train in
a dream or a nightmare, he has his ticket, he doesn't have
his ticket, he asks an employee how long the crossing takes,
maybe he will have time upon arriving to go to the barber's,
she points out the presence of Zuckerkrönchen in the enormous room of the restaurant where more Jews are eating
than he has ever seen in his whole life, thousands, unfortunately he doesn't see the one who is the heart of his heart
but the idea that she is right then eating German pastries
nourishes him, she eats while stretching her arm out at a
regular rhythm like an automaton, it hits you in the face that
she is of the same manufacture as Olympia the daughter of
Coppelius and Andreas of the family of Nathanael, naturally
it is I who sees what Andreas does not see. I note moreover
that since I have been following my family relations, by force
of imagining them up close, I enter and exit for the past several weeks I come and go without difficulty, more and more
familiarly, internally, I learn more every day about all these
people, but not only, I also have a fair number of things to
teach them, I have several keys of my own confided by Ève.
    There are also the dreams where he misses the train,

he arrives running along the platform, encumbered by a
weighty guilt, fear of missing the train, or of catching it, it's
his travel rug that made him late, he couldn't find it, he
is ashamed, he has the vague sensation that there is a link
between the rug and Irmgard. Life is a station, he repeats to
himself, he seeks and does not see. Absurd thoughts cross his
mind, this one for example: if only I had a cat, or a rabbit,
or a hen, someone who would love me and whom I could
caress with my fingertips in the night and who would caress
with the tip of her fur or feathers but Else will never accept
an animal in the house, even a guinea pig of the least little
thing she is jealous.

Why then would he miss the train because of the rug?
what secrets does he hide from himself under the rug? yet
another question one would like to have been able to ask
Dr. Freud, a desire (that of asking questions) that my uncle
André has hidden all his life while thinking about it all the
time, to the point of wanting to weep the day he passed down
Berggasse in front of padlocked number 19 on Else's arm
being careful not to dent his air of indifference and now it
is too late, to die without ever having understood why his
fears always realized his desires, which led him finally to go
to Jerusalem like a condemned man who has misread his
order, seems to him an unbearable punishment

One time he left behind his lot of submissive and condemned
man, this too deserves an explanation, it was when he had
a violent and totally out-of-character argument with Kolkmeyer, the watchmaker. It was already before '33, already in
'28 perhaps it was that Kolkmeyer began to take photos of
Jewish stores and persons, innocent clients guilty of betray-
ing their blood and that of Kolkmeyer who went into these
Jewish stores, one never knew when one went to consult Dr.
Pelz or make some purchases at Wertheim's, whether, upon

going out one was not going to be *photographed* by Kolk-meyer and suddenly such an anger, coming from the high-est antiquity, roused Andreas and he yelled at Kolkmeyer "You are a moron!" and Frau Kolkmeyer cast a poisonous look at him (the fatal look cast at Colonel Chabert by Lady Chapotel) and she spit out: "You, that doesn't make anyone want to come near you!" And Onkel André felt in his breast that he blamed himself even as he approved of what he had done. But indignation always has a bitter taste. On the wall of Grossestrasse he "saw," in a true hallucination, his death sentence. There was thus someone in Osnabrück who would feel a savage and personal joy in cutting off his head. Then he leaves for Palestine by that station and that train, and he laughs up his sleeve: he was going to surprise Irmgard over there, and here, which he leaves forever, there is someone who will be amazed tomorrow and it's Kolkmeyer whom he has deprived of his prey.

THERE IS PALESTINE AND PALESTINE, the Steins' and the Jonases'. To me, fate has fobbed off a pitiless Palestine, which boycotts old people and which, yet another absurd thought, in certain cases resembled that country where they eliminate the handicapped, thinks Andreas. If the watchmaker only knew! Yet another question: did Onkel André refuse to leave for Chile to rejoin Hans Gunther? Did he want to leave for Chile? What are the external obstacles and the internal obstacles that resulted in Onkel André not going to Chile? What is the relation between the two mirages, the daughter-mirage and the son-mirage? One heads to the Orient the other the Occident as if the offspring put distance itself between them. Did Hans Gunther *want to leave* for Chile? or did he *not want to leave* for Jerusalem? Is there anyone to answer the questions that loom before the Book? And what does Gustav Stein think of the journey Osnabrück-Jerusalem-and-back of his friend? And what does Andreas say when he returns to his several friends? But no one is listening to him. People are preoccupied enough as it is with their *exit*, every week they read job offers, in all the countries of the world where people are ready to hire German Jewish specialists or Jewish Germans who can furnish reliable recommendations.

CIRCULAR 5

On the basis of information that the foreign committees have sent us recently, we are passing along to you a list of jobs for which it is possible to apply. We request that you ask any possible candidates to send us their application including a curriculum vitae, copies of their recommendations, and information about the funds at their disposal.

• The chair of chemistry at the University of Madrid seeks two chemists who can present excellent recommendations, one of which must be a specialist in the fabrication of insulin, the other a specialist in the fabrication of salvarsan. If we can recommend men who meet the requirements, it seems possible that they can be accepted immediately.

• In England, we may have the possibility of obtaining work permits for:

– an optical technician (conception of optical lenses, systems, and devices). The latter will have responsibility for producing devices conceived on the basis of optical data of a new kind, which is why only the candidacy of a highly qualified expert with excellent knowledge in all theoretical and practical domains will be considered.

– experts in the process of potassium cyanide extraction of gold from crushed gravel.

– experts in the process of oil flow for the extraction of other metals from crushed gravel.

– experts in dairy products (casein).

• In Barcelona, a highly qualified film projectionist is sought.

• In Amsterdam, a polisher of gemstones is sought (please contact by telegram!) as well as a tailor of leather garments.

• In Oslo (Norway), a lady seeks to sell her enterprise. A sensible entrepreneur could earn his living and possibly support many, possibly in connection with furniture manufacture.

• In England, there is demand for service personnel, the type of personnel most often needed and that is, relatively, the best paid. However, such employment entails work that is carried out in the basement, a uniform must be worn, and friendly relations with the English service personnel are expected.

• In Holland, a doctor, who wishes to and can serve as optician and surgical truss maker, could find work. Salary: 30 florins per week. Kindly send copies of recommendations immediately.

• In Brussels, the following positions are empty at the School of Applied Sciences:

– the chair of Technology of vegetal products.

– the chair of General Electricity and Electricity Transmission including the direction of the Laboratory of electrical measurements.

Candidates must not undertake direct application but contact us.

• A note from the Parisian committee informs us that it is possible to find positions for qualified custom tailors, who must be able, however, to meet the requirements of Parisian taste.

• In Paris, there is an opening for a builder of technical cleaning installations who has particular experience in the construction of containers and piping. Remuneration 1,500 francs per month.

• In The Hague, an opening for a young woman who knows shorthand in German, French, and English.

• A report on the possibilities of settling in Spanish Morocco indicates that doctors can find rather good opportunities there. First of all, as concerns language, the knowledge of Spanish is desired but French can suffice if necessary.

Men can earn their living from the first day, as one says, and would also fulfill a particular education function. In

principle, the climate in Tetuan is excellent, however, because of the lack of hygiene in the Mellah, tuberculosis is
widespread. This is probably linked to sudden temperature
changes, accompanied by colds, and also to the dust. For
Jewish doctors then a vast field of work would open up in the
teaching of hygiene measures. The fight against the periodic
presence of malaria can also play a role.

There is a dentist in Tetuan. As concerns other parts of
the Spanish zone, we believe it is possible to find satisfactory
positions for:

 – a doctor and a dentist in Larache
 – a doctor in Xauen
 – a doctor in Alcazar, and perhaps as well
 – a doctor in Axcila

More detailed information is forthcoming, thus this information is provisional.

Moreover, we would likely be able to place 1 or 2 pharma-
cists. A capable engineer, even if he has little capital, could
fabricate numerous necessary small industrial objects.

1–2 automobile mechanics or workmen could likewise
earn their living.

A Hebrew teacher with a university degree and able to
pronounce Hebrew with a Sephardic accent would be wel-
come for teaching the young. He should also be capable of
proposing a suitable teaching of the Talmud. Thanks to the
extraordinary desire to succeed among some young people,
it is a question of very satisfying work, which, moreover,
would not be badly remunerated, around 400–500 pesetas,
for the moment.

For Spanish Morocco, candidacies of a qualified cabi-
netmaker, a blacksmith, and a milliner will also be considered.

 • In Holland, we have perhaps the possibility of placing
people who work in film (cameramen, assistant directors,

actors). Such candidates are asked to send us copies of their recommendations.

• From Barcelona we have received information that a qualified craftsman in machine weaving of cotton and silk is sought. The candidacy of someone who can bring a capital of 2,000–10,000 pesetas and who could thus be welcomed as partner will be given preference.

A housemaid, who has excellent cooking skills, is also sought.

Upon reading these circulars, the candidates from Osnabrück are overcome by the ambivalent exhilaration that is aroused in us at the sight of the "genealogical tree" of Balzac's *Human Comedy*: innumerable possibilities of an individual or family novel are offered to them. They see in the distant year 2000 their great-grandchildren working in a hospital in Shanghai or having rapidly made a fortune managing a supermarket in Johannesburg, and simultaneously they see themselves dying of malaria having barely set foot in Morocco.

Such a superabundance of possible biographies arouses in them either an exaltation or a paralysis. And there is also for some of them the idea of going to that underdeveloped part of the Middle East administered by England that attracts some young people and repels many people from Osnabrück, for there, no ambiguity, if you go there, to Palestine, you know in advance that you will be first of all and forever Jewish, the country decides for you, which is not the case if you go to Montevideo, whereas until now one has been German and an Osnabrücker. The perspective of *becoming* another is a torment that no candidate escapes, that is to say, to disinvest from one day to the next the (German) becoming in which one had installed one's habits of being, one's language, one's memory since the beginning of one's memory, with the familiar characters of one's memory, from the Kaiser to Liebknecht, Brüning, the whole Goethian fashioning of all points of view, in order to leap into a totally unknown mental combination, and thus to feel the particular pain that accompanies every metamorphosis, makes more than one vacillate and even shrivel up. It's like drinking an alchemical potion and undergoing an operation of grieving for the whole person, a horror, for one was attached to oneself.

Here I am trying to answer the question: how to explain that some people cannot manage to say to themselves that they cannot manage to resolve from one day to the next to cease being German, since they are or believed they are?

How to explain that that year (1935), so many people leave while he alone comes back, such that for a moment one has the impression that the whole Jewish world flew off its branch with one beat of their wings, that is to say, two hundred at one blow?

It's destiny. Sometimes an event lends a hand to destiny in one sense or in another. For example the demonstration that summer that brought thirty thousand people together on the theme *Osnabrück and the Jewish Question*, that's not what incited certain families (Jewish-declared) to pack their bags, but the fact that the mayor defined this meeting of thirty thousand people, which is to say, all-Osnabrück-together-as-a-family, as *Action of Enlightenment*. But other families (declared Jewish) let this storm pass. There are those who left immediately, and those that ended up leaving, and those who did not leave. I would have difficulty imagining these latter ones if I were not enlightened by the story of Onkel

André. There are those who don't know how to swim or ride a bicycle and who have no occupation, in place of an occupation there is the argument of family (Jewish-declared), that is the case of Omi my grandmother who might have found it indecent to leave before her older brother and go to Africa was that better, on the Race question?

A cousin is a nurse in Berlin, she believes that she believes she is indispensable at her hospital, that is what she wants to believe and to make her two young children believe, we won't speak of the husband, no one will ever say what his "specialty" is, and despite this special "specialty," which is ruinous and monomaniacal, the cousin believes she is indispensable also to the special man who suffers as truly as Dostoevsky in Roulettenberg. They do not leave. People come to get them. Destiny assigns them a journey that is a geopolitical curiosity: a train takes them to the north of Germany in the south of France, as if Gurs were German, in order to put them again in a train going north that passes through Drancy to take them to Auschwitz. While Gerda is at Gurs, almost the whole year of '40–'41, then at the Port Terminal in Marseille for almost the whole of the year '42, my mother painted Oran to her in glowing colors, and in vain. For all of this is decided by that mix of History and bad choice that is the leavening of Greek tragedy.

My mother prevents me from telling everything, there is worse, there is worse. She does not want the worst to be known, and yet she is the one who told me the worst, she herself did not succeed in not telling it.

THE NOTE WHISPERS. —I, the note, am going to whisper what H. cannot say. So first Gerda and her husband the poker player, who moreover was not bothered that he had a squint and bewitched his wife, are deportiert Gurs–Drancy–Auschwitz. But the two little children are spirited away by an underground association, and kept alive by a Jewish association. That is when the deassociation happens: Ger's sister, who lives in New York, on the one hand adopts the boy on the other hand does not adopt the girl. The girl remains.

—And why? why? whispers H.

—She didn't have room in her apartment, says Ève with the large serene eyes.

—No room for the girl? cries H.

—A little apartment, says Ève with the large eyes.

Oh Oh Oh!

You hear that? It's H. stomping her foot. Oh! Oh! I keep silent. Get out of my book! she cries. I dissipate into the paper. Pretend I didn't whisper anything.

numbers, numbers, prophetic warnings of the depths
 of the present
Tell me
What I do not know
How many souls on the edge of the black?
Count out the souls for me
prophets of the black tales
Show me what I do not see

But sometimes it happens that I suspect there is perhaps still
worse than this worst that my mother whispered to me

How many characters are there in Balzac's Human Comedy?

—That's really a hard question, says my daughter. Three hundred four hundred perhaps?

—Another hard question, I say: how many Jews were there in Osnabrück in the '30s? —Five thousand? says my daughter. —Two thousand, says my son. —How many characters in the *Odyssey*? —It's been an eternity since I read it. They say.

Do you want the answers?

There are four hundred thirty-five characters, and perhaps fewer in my six-bit odyssey of Osnabrück, I say. No! exclaims my daughter and me too, and you too, we all say: four hundred thirty-five or something like that! but that's nothing! four hundred out of or next to — ninety-five thousand? A few families (declared-Jewish) and thirty thousand Osnabrückers who bark: "Germans! We must wake up! The Jews have bitten us!" That August 20, 1935, the Cathedral square is black with the Chorus of the anguished Pure: Germans, rise up! Come to the Aid of German Blood! What strikes us is the disproportion that is perhaps the occult figure of an equivalence: on the one side thirty thousand plus the mayor, on the other four hundred thirty-five, it is not the hounding of the infinitesimal, thinks Public Opinion of Osnabrück, it demonstrates clearly the hidden power of foreign bodies: it took all the living strength of the City to repulse the attack, only the German elderly, those under five years old, and sick people were not involved in the struggle against the Jewishquestion. Whoever says *one* Jew says *invasion*, we are exorcising just in time.

— And in the *Odyssey*?

— Between three hundred forty and four hundred thirty-five, I say.

— Oh! That's enormous! says my daughter.

— There is four hundred thirty-five and four hundred thirty-five, I say.

— There were so many characters when one listened to Ève's stories, says my son, there was the whole world, one starts with one character from Osnabrück and by following the network of interrelations, from one individual to another, one arrives in Ithaca, it's the evening of life, almost all are dead.

Yet one more belief that goes up in smoke: in Oran Osnabrück was a great City containing many cities among which flourished an important Jewish city that naturally was agnostic, the greater part of the tens of thousands of Jews of Osnabrück were *gemütlich*, Jewish for the holidays, were no longer strictly Jewish, were Jewish lightly, joyfully, with tennis swimming socialism medical studies to come in Köln or Berlin, seen from my mother's stories, it was Paris in Lower Saxony and I had no idea as to the epic difference. Three hundred ninety-four in 1934 out of ninety-eight thousand? If there hadn't been the dome on the synagogue one would not even have known *where* to catch sight of them. For so few, there was not even a rabbi, they make do with a Kantor, and a reciter who moreover may be Abraham Jonas or Andreas Jonas. And no beards. With that one can in fact unfold the eighteen acts of the *Odyssey*.

On another side I imagine the dark red resentment of Kolkmeyer who, from his point of view, only had ever a small flock to slaughter, impossible to get the numbers up, an injustice of fate, whereas in the other cities of Hanover or Westphalia one all the same went up to a thousand if not five or six thousand. He even thought about going to plunder the neighboring towns. But on another side *so few* is a lot and it is too much. If they are "so few" it's because they proliferate in secret, with the help of the camera moreover one can multiply them both with enlargements and conversely by displaying in his watchmaker-jeweler's window such small photos that passersby *had to* come closer and peer in order to see, what's more by decreasing the size, one augments the natural disgust for this species of insects. Four hundred! That's enormous! one just has to imagine two in every street, a couple, and the entire city is infested. That's enough! Osnabrück invaded by four hundred seventeen Jews! Imagine four thousand one hundred and seventy, and the city is swallowed up, says Kolkmeyer, and people imagined.

Look at the photos: you see? What's more, they are not bearded. They dress as do the bourgeois of Osnabrück, like all their true victims the true bourgeois of Osnabrück, at *Wertheim Deutsche Herren Mode*, two steps away from Kolkmeyer's watchmaker-jewelry shop.

And me too in Oran, when I look at the photo albums of Osnabrück, I found them, all the gentlemen of our families, elegant, refined, they had the crafty blue gaze and the air of modern bourgeois that foretold the European Germany to come. My mother too, Omi too, and their fifty-year head start over France.

O admirable power of phantasm, I say to myself, political force, factory of realities that are more solid than natural synthetic realities. Kolkmeyer was also very attached to the power of phantasm. When at Christmas he made posters proclaiming *Christliche Weihnacht = Jüdischer Verdienst.* Jews are advancing. Soon Germans will no longer be able to lodge in Osnabrück. After fifty years of Jews, *lebt der schaffende Deutsche Mensch demnach in Hinterhäusern und Keller Wohnungen* — and he was the first one to believe it. It was not a lie, it was fiction become true. Germans being driven into basements and backyard sheds, behind the J.s, the Jewish shop.

What Kolkmeyer thought when, at the corner of Grosse-strasse and Nikolaiort, he came upon Andreas Jonas returned not like a revenant, but really alive: "As if he had spit in his face. And what's more, they come back." Kolkmeyer could not understand Andreas. That Andreas Jonas wasn't pallid, trembling. Nor courageous. *Indifferent*, that's the word. Whereas Dr. Pelz, that very dignified and apparently self-controlled gentleman when his daughter Anna was taken away from him to be deported, there was in his eyes the sort of horror that sprang into the right eye of Gloucester when his left eye was torn out and he said nothing. And if Andreas had had a daughter to be taken away, Kolkmeyer would certainly have tried.

But I am going astray. For the *indifference*, Kolkmeyer had no explanation.

That Andreas had lost in Palestine the taste for rage and hatred, that since his journey he inhabited a world beyond Osnabrück-Jerusalem where no one could reproach anyone anything, because wickedness evil fault were equally distributed there among all individuals, there was no longer any difference, neither inferiority nor superiority, no one knew it.

"Irmgard killed me but it is not a crime, it's an infirmity, she lacks the organ called pity, or love, it is not her fault, there are causes in me, there are others in god," Andreas tries to think, but this wearies him, there are things that one can never manage to explain, it is what Job used to say, from there a kind of resignation to everything that one doesn't understand, beginning with oneself and thus one's neighbor, the result of this chain of inexplicables is that he notices he no longer has the *taste* for hatred toward Kolkmeyer and his Nazi colleagues.

What happened to Kolkmeyer? That's a question that comes late, and only on the occasion of my trip to Osnabrück. Since he existed in reality, it is possible, if his family was not extinguished and annihilated like the Jonas family, and if it prospered, as a result of this double fact, it is possible that his dreams were realized, that his shop expanded, it is possible that the Kolkmeyer family pursued the same positive progression as the City. I imagine that the history of the shop gives them work or worries or perhaps satisfaction, the Kolkmeyers. But I don't want to go any further in this direction. It's useless. With the internet the reserve stocks of imagination and secrecy are greatly diminished. Those of the emotions, surprises, passions, all the affects that are the engines of tragedy or of comedytragedy are also limited by the stupefying spread of information. I prefer to have the freedom of fiction. Right here, then, I invent that Kolkmeyer's granddaughter married a Russian Jewish mathematician whom she met at University. Nothing prevents one from thinking that it is perhaps true. Starting from this little

event one could go back in the Kolkmeyer family to the day
in October '35 when Kolkmeyer plans to have done with
the Jonases without realizing that the one he sees on the
platform is in truth dead.

On that autumn day in 1935, it is not raining, the colors
of the trees sparkle and Ève does not know that for dozens of
years she will not have the pleasure of watching the work of
this beautiful season, for there is no autumn in Oran. She
arrived at the station in the famous train of the photo. She
has come to convince her mother to follow her, to leave
Germany. —Es ist Zeit. "Kann ich nicht," says Omi. What is
Rosi doing all alone in Osnabrück? Or else she wasn't alone?
The Engers? Are getting ready to leave. Do they know? If
yes, have they said so? It had to be a very strong bond of
attachment for her to resist the arms, the hand, the voice
of Ève. There are many things I don't understand. I prefer
to think that Omi my grandmother was held back by a secret
stronger than her daughter and for which she was ready to
risk her life. I always thought of her as old, but she was only
fifty-three at the time.

   One thing I know, and that no one else in the world
knows, is that Ève also met Baruth that day, for the last time,
at that period, but for the last time of the story that no one
will know if I don't tell it. Moreover Baruth always suffered
from a suffering all his own. He suffered from having lost
the faith *that he had never had*. He would have liked to have
once known the taste of it. Here's a real case: I'm talking
about a charming, cultivated, touching man, and not a
negligible one since when he arrives in 1930, he takes up
the role of minimumrabbi, of pseudorabbi, of backuprabbi,
of replacement, discount rabbi in the absence of a for-real
rabbi, and fortunately it was understood that he was only

playing this role because Artur, that's his name, had inconveniently lost his faith, which no one ever knew except my mother. That explains that he could read the prayers but although a Preacher he could not preach. In spite of his efforts to fulfill his contract. Ève went to the synagogue out of affection for Artur who loved her. And in the middle of the sermon, Artur was totally lost: no more voice, no more memory, no more will to play, and it was painful for everyone. Those who had faith, and Ève and Baruth who did not, everyone had a lump in their throat, it was awful. In the archives, the entry for Baruth is the most succinct of all the entries. It is reported (*Stationen*, p. 21) that:

"Artur Baruth was an eminent personality, very well educated. He came from Berlin. Otherwise not much is known about him, except the year of his death: he died in 1936."

There is no photo.

He offered to my Ève, to my *rêve*, volumes of poetry in French. He had been a salesman before, but he didn't sell anything because after having made his pitch he had such a warm relationship with his listeners that he no longer dared to make them pay.

That autumn day Ève told Artur that she is now engaged. It was a day of last times. In place of a photo the archives show a facsimile of a page from the contract drawn up for two years between the Osnabrück community and Mr. Artur Baruth as Lehrer, Kantor and Prediger, and signed by him and by the representative of the community, Jonas.

Andreas Jonas felt an inexpressible sympathy for the young man who lost his way in the middle of his sermons. The one and the other had had one of those visions of mortified humanity that Kierkegaard speaks of. One does not get over it. The one or the other could not believe two words of what he said.

Yes, Onkel André on the platform, in the photo, one sees that he is dreaming, anachronistic.

Baruth as well had always been anachronistic. In a hyperrealist period without future he died as he lived and vice versa, died in a novel, like a character out of Döblin, clueless, with brio and misery, and not in a concentration camp, but in a hospital, struck down by TB and all alone, all the friends have left. Ève gets married in Algeria, god too has left, the synagogues look like cellar vaults, through an opening of the door large brown dogs make as if to enter, the author yells: "no! get out!" but in any case there is no longer anyone in the empty cavity.

If this were a novel and not the result of a private collision, he (Baruth) would be followed in these last pages by the nurse who believed so strongly she was indispensable to the survival of her patients that she did not see that the hospital "opened" by the back door onto the concentration camp. Thanks to her care one had a chance to die cured, says my mother. Or else she dressed up in a white gown the social dissidence of her spouse, whose total commitment to the game of poker sheltered from the advice lavished by fear.

But this book is not a fictional novel, it is the bruise caused by the shock produced between the City and the indefinite self, with all my books by its side and seventy years of Homeric stories proffered by my mother, and incidentally by my aunt and my grandmother, such that by following them I have wandered for a hundred years with giants through all the lands. A shock of surprise and love.

Among the three hundred ninety-four or four hundred thirty-five characters, the highest number reached just one year in this six-bit epic, Baruth will have been the most eminent of the abandonables, the poorest of the tenants, and the most powerfully comic. That is why he figures in such a lapidary fashion in the archives, like a quickly stifled joke. Yet for the vigilant consciousness of the rare survivors and descendants of the inhuman years, it is fitting to present oneself before the public, the spectators to be conquered, with a serious demeanor, which testifies to the dignity that emanates from such a frightful catastrophe, that is why responsible persons have the instinctive wisdom that urges them to filter the characters discreetly. By instinct the clown is pushed aside, but one must not say so, at least for some years to come.

I understand that during the hundred years after the unnamable outburst of humans and the incomprehensible extravagance of the god of Job, after the time without the skin of pity, the poets who approach, and must approach, the cruel land might be commanded to avoid the faults of taste that could damage the right to unconditional respect for all those who suffered directly or obliquely because of the structural injustice of destiny. Nothing, not a comma, any longer separated scholars scoundrels rapists charitable and honest people bandits were no longer but a single family of those tortured beneath the blows of fate. And then it was indeed necessary to love one another without regard for antipathies, that was the only solution so as not to furnish the devil with ammunition, and keep the secrets locked up for at least seventy-five years, preferably one hundred. What happened or didn't happen at Osnabrück's Synagogue, for example, must-not-be-said before 2038, that on every Shabbat god again gave Baruth the proof that he didn't exist, he interrupted his speech, put blanks in his sermon, not to mention the inadvertent "spoonerisms" as my mother used to call them, subjected him to ridicule and gave him stomachaches, my mother used to tell me this while doubling up with laughter beneath the seal of secrecy, and why did

Artur Baruth persist in being this unhappy divine salesman incapable of selling spiritual dry goods and suspenders, it couldn't have been for the minimum-wage salary of 4,200 R.M. a year?

During one hundred years people will have expected from the poets that they observe the truce and the mourning period and that everything that begins with J- ends naturally with just.

Perhaps I should not have
come to Osnabrück?

One departs from Osnabrück

Despite the strikes that petrify the trains throughout
germany, I leave Osnabrück, the return from Osnabrück
is included in the dream, this time the train will not go
through Essen but Köln. Strike rhymes with dreamlike, says
my mother.

It was a dream chasing a dream. A miracle-dream and a
reality-dream. I admit, I do not deny, this time I believe I
have been to Osnabrück.

Before Osnabrück I was wondering what would happen
to me upon contact with Osnabrück. In Osnabrück nothing
happened, nothing has happened, the Present controlled
my thinking in its authoritarian and realist manner, it was
2015, I was calling up forcefully 1935, last presence already
withdrawn of Ève in her childhood city, I took her image
from 1928, she had just cut her hair, she had come to cut the
last ties, I made her walk at a lively pace, we passed in front
of the Dom, we rushed down the narrow witches' alley, it
was at the Hase, the little sparkling Hase,
      that I could contemplate time with Ève,

I am seeking, I am seeking you, I am seeking what you were seeking. I felt that we were leaving, I felt her leaving (it's only when coming), I felt I was leaving

As for me, already in Osnabrück, I had left, the train leaves at 1:37 in the afternoon, but at nine a.m. I had already left, I seemed to be there out of politeness, but Osnabrück and I no longer had much to say to each other.

Maman was no longer there. She had left long ago and more than once. She had left freely in 1929, in total freedom, she exited Osnabrück Hanover, she set her course toward the world, and with that, she had saved me.

One leaves Osnabrück. One cannot not have a fondness for Osnabrück. Osnabrück doesn't have an overblown idea of itself, says Ève. It knows and does not say. It knows it is a city from which one departs, after the Abitur, one leaves it, that is its destiny. It's a city where one has one's childhood, one grows up. Once the rounds of Osnabrück are done, one takes one's leave.

Osnabrück is rather proud of its celebrities. It doesn't boast of them. It thanks them, it's an honor, no one ever imagined that E. M. Remarque or Felix Nussbaum or my mother could remain in Osnabrück after having obtained the Abitur. Osnabrück always expected these detachments. It's natural. It is a good nurse for little ones and then for the dead.

The duck glides on the Hase, followed, no, *preceded* by ten little peeping ones and right away after before, they take off, they pedal at a dizzying pace, they speed up past their mother

—What was I expecting when I decided to go to Osnabrück? I asked myself.

I was sitting a thousand miles southwest of Osnabrück in the garden with, in the neighboring armchair, the "Presence" of Ève at my side as usual, and the cats on the other side, it was she who in me was questioning me, I cast a look around us, and I swear that I saw the square tower of the Dom in the grand avenue, we were here, a thousand miles away from Osnabrück and we were on the little metal bridge over the Hase it could not be denied, I saw us.

—I really don't know what I expected, I say, so much time and so many people crowded around me. I have forgotten

Perhaps I expected long ago that to my mother would be restored a part of her memorial properties, but she herself didn't want them, no property, no goods, perhaps not. When I presented myself to the City, it happens that what it offered me is the tragedy of Onkel André, which I was not claiming, but the book inherited it.

I did not expect the existence of a Bürgermeisterin cut from a piece of cloth of the Enlightenment. She was posted there where Fraulein von Längecke had really existed. I said to the Bürgermeisterin on the one hand the Jews are humans-therefore, therefore-equal and alike-in-evil-and-not-evil to all humans, and on the other hand, as I was passing down Grossestrasse before the watchmaker-jewelry shop, I thought in the end there is no longer in Osnabrück a single Jewish Mitbürger from Osnabrück, but the Kolkmeyer shop window has gotten much bigger, and you don't see photos in the foreground, I didn't have time to go in if I had had time I would have gone in, at least I tell myself, I should have gone in, I would have planted an apple tree in their garden, I should have restarted creation from zero.

Perhaps among all the unknown reasons for going to Osnabrück, where good and evil grow together on the apple tree, I had wanted to see where, in what décor, in which streets, in what music of language my mother's life, and subsequently mine, had begun to be interpellated, declared, then convoked by the word Jew,

where, in what landscape, in what climate, on what occasion or date or season, I had lost, before my birth, rights: the rights of the self, the right to be-Jewish and to be-notJewish at will, at my will, according to my desire, whenever I felt like it. And every time the word presents itself and says to me: you! I say: yes, I cannot not say yes, even if at that moment I am a cat or two or a book or a king or a squirrel I say: yes, because one *must* respond, one must not leave the scene where the massacre has taken place because of the word, because of the thirst for blood and hatred, just as you, you can't stop being Khmer or Armenian, or — one is *obliged*, at least during the centuries when the ghosts are still at their posts.

When I thus-went there, the week before I was not Jewish I was Burmese and I was just beginning to become anti-imperialist, but already the day before, and that morning, at the train station, I felt that I was going to Osnabrück as a Jew, the word was waiting for me, you! I stood up and I followed, I was going there as a Jew and also as nonJew, I represented the two complementary aspects, thus as Jew-it-depends, as woman and daughter and also Jew as daughter of my mother from Osnabrück.

And as poet I read in the streets and on the sidewalks what my mother and Omi *could not* tell me with their own mouths, because they are sworn to the family and to the people and they do not dare break their oath. An impossibility to which Literature, which is my other family and my other people, opposes its rights. For example the right not to hide that, in front of the apple tree of pity and cruelty, every human being is equal to every human being so long as she/he has not made her/his choice.

"*I HAVE THE IMPRESSION SOMETIMES OF BEING MYSELF THE GHOST OF AN EMPTY SYNAGOGUE* but only apparently, for nothing is more crowded with ghosts than a synagogue ghost," says the book. "I am in the same state as Baruth when he entered the synagogue having been deprived of the aid of faith: he was measured, the poor man, against the enormous absence of god. God has a crushing inexistence."

Since I went to Osnabrück an unforeseen throng has been produced in me. There is an incredible crowd. To think I believed — did I believe it? — that I would find only my adored mother, with her sister and her mother! And now there hurries toward me a crowd of people who are half-buried, half-lost, as soon as I turn toward one the other comes too, each one refers to his or her neighbor, I pronounce a name, twenty people come forward

my vital solitude is threatened, I am more and more worried,

But I never intended to lodge so many people in my mental space, I am not a hotel, I fear being unable to refuse hospitality, and from there politeness and from there sympathy and, insidious, confusion with others.

—Not-talking-about-it has been one of the laws of this history, says my daughter.

—And why? I say.

—That's a good question.

—I have to ask it of Inès from Chile. But I don't have her number. I don't even have her name. She must have been called Jonas in the past but I'm not sure.

—Inès, what would her Osnabrück name have been? says my daughter.

The Jonases no sooner shipwrecked than originally-Chileans, I say. Likewise there were Jonases no sooner shipwrecked than originally-Brazilians and the Jonases of Uruguay.

—For children-who-survived of parents who barely survived, says my daughter, an unbearable pain and a source of guilt, says my daughter.

—And why? I say.

—The child, says my daughter, does not want to be hurt. She feels guilty of feeling that she does not want to inherit the parental horror, he feels guilty resenting his parents for having been hurt, the parents are afraid that their children will balk at their destiny of children of unhappy parents, it's in Balzac, the child resents the parents, principally the father, for being the cause that he feels guilty for resenting those to whom he is born-attached, for having had the misfortune of being unfortunate.

—One no longer speaks of it, I say. In any case not in Spanish or in English. All of this happened in German.

—They no longer speak German, except for the accent.

—Speak German! I used to say to Ève. I would put Ève and Éri together in the living room and I would say to them: speak German! And then I'd say it in English: Please! Speak

German! They would try. Fortunately they argued in German. But if I relaxed my surveillance they would get on board English, believing, they said, that it was in a German train that they were speaking to each other. I was afraid of losing our language.

Fortunately, I say, when Omi arrived in Oran in November 1938, on the one hand she had all her German baggage, her German angers, her indignant German explosions and the piercing German blue looks she cast, on the other hand and fortunately she spoke not a word of French, and with her whole German character she caused to enter our apartment at least two hundred German words, and perhaps four hundred words, armed and incandescent. It's been a long time since I heard her riddle the air with her Omi words. But on the edge of Oblivion, I concentrate, not a day goes by that I don't retrieve one of these vigorous words. The morning I took back *Schlimm*. Such a little person, four foot nine, and her interior world: a maelstrom.

And I add *Schlimm* to the list of stormy words from Osnabrück that keeps getting longer in my notebook, not far from *ekelhaft*, *grässlich*, and *widerlich*.

—According to me, it is the victims who fear not being up to the elevated position in which fate has *cast* them *over and above* the common fate, and thus they endeavor to dress up the faults and impurities of their *Opfer* soul. Not-to-speak-of-it is a minimal precaution against imperfections.

—The two old lady cousins from Los Angeles, says my daughter, survivors of Auschwitz, who had husbands who died in the camp, who married other camp survivors, who didn't last, they had a supernatural gaiety, they had a cage of canaries and they played dominos.

—Or else the canaries and the dominos served as a mask

for the abscesses of the soul. Or else they had been changed into canaries.

—Enough! says my mother. We will speak of it no more.

Perhaps I should not have
gone to Osnabrück.

Was Inès from Chile the daughter of Hans Gunther? Or of Kurt? And of Omi's two sisters who were deported to Theresienstadt, who is left, where, is there someone in New Zealand or in South Africa who still exclaims *das ist schlimm!* with the intonation of Osnabrück?

It occurs to me that perhaps I had to leave Osnabrück in order to go to Jerusalem, perhaps the City is the Kristall door through which I must pass in order to go to Jerusalem. It seems to me that it's from Osnabrück that came the order for me to go to Jerusalem where I didn't want to go, it seems to me that it's under the sway of Osnabrück City-of-Peace that it became obligatory and fated for me to go there. But I'm afraid of mistaking my feeling for a true event.

—Was I pushed, obscurely of course, toward Jerusalem by the idea that Marga is left, that perhaps Marga has not yet died there, that perhaps she is still alive, still speaks, which is improbable, objectively, because she is as old as Ève, and at one hundred and five years old my mother speaks to me only internally now? I wondered.

—Absolutely not, says the book. I am witness.

AND NOW IN JERUSALEM? YOU ARE THERE? A little, if one can call it being there, I am a little, a little displaced, I move a half-inch off the ground, no one sees a half-inch, it's this slight discrepancy that makes me wobble, this infinitesimal contraction of incredulity, I am not the only one who is surprised, everyone asks me how it is that I accepted to go to Jerusalem, my friends at Hebrew University are astonished, those who asked me to come cannot get over it, but what does that mean, "to accept"? I remember: when I decided to go to Osnabrück, I subsequently accepted to go to Jerusalem with the thought that I wouldn't go, that this trip would not happen, at the last minute the hunter Gracchus's little boat misses the junction, no one knows why, I make my way with my daughter along the vast and long corridor where dangers of all sorts are lurking, Algerian vases, photo albums that are taken away before our eyes and pulled up at the end of a rope through a hole in the ceiling, at the end of the tunnel we go left, but it's a dead end, we ought to have gone right, the wandering is indefinite and when finally we

124

land on Mount Moriah, there is a doubt, there was indeed a place, but I was in back, I was late I was still not where I was, I was all askew.

My mother also asks me how it is that I accepted to go to Jerusalem, you are not a Zionist, you're going to argue with everyone, as for me, says my mother, I didn't go there, myself I could have gone to see Marga, but once she moved to Jerusalem after having lived in London and Belfast, she too does not want to go elsewhere to see me, and now that I am no longer there you accept to go? — It's because I didn't want to go there, I say. When I don't want, I go against my will — So go ahead. But I don't know if you are going to arrive.

—I will arrive there, I say, but perhaps not in this book

Here ends the book of Osnabrück, just in front of Mount Moriah. The book of Jerusalem had already begun.

—Is this your first time in Jerusalem? the Superdirector of the Museum of Israel asks me.

—I have already been to Jerusalem, I say, but I forgot. It is thus my first time in Jerusalem.

From the very little terrace at the top of the Mount of Olives I saw the whole book that I will write later.

—And the catastrophe that happened to you at the Wailing Wall, that unbelievable thing, you don't want to tell it here?

—No, no. I will write it later. The later I write it the more the metamorphosis will have progressed.

—And what if you forget?

THE END

HIER WOHNTE
ANDREAS JONAS
JG. 1869
DEPORTIERT JULI 1942
THERESIENSTADT
ERMORDET 6.9.1942

HIER WOHNTE
ELSE JONAS
JG. 1880
DEPORTIERT JULI 1942
THERESIENSTADT
ERMORDET 25.1.1944

When, after the end of the book, I find Inès from Chile, I telephone her, how good it is to hear from you she says, and she tells me that she is nearing her end, she fears. We speak hastily, on the scale of the short time we have remaining, it seems to us. She answers me directly, as if we were filling out the last questionnaire together. Her father was indeed Hans Gunther Jonas. She was born in '48 in Chile, her father died in '75. Did he speak to her of Osnabrück? of his childhood?

—Never never never.

—Did she ask him questions?

—Never never. They didn't speak of their interior life, the parents. It was taboo at the time. In Chile also, taboo.

When I ask her if she knows any of the Jonas descendants (those of the eight Jonas brothers and sisters of whom Andreas was the eldest and of whom, although many of them disappeared in several different concentration camps, an equal number survived the shipwreck and found themselves thrown onto distant shores, some in Chile, in Brazil, in Uruguay, others in South Africa, in Australia, in New Zealand, some in England, in Ireland, in the USA, someone in Shanghai), she says simply: "I knew no one. I don't know my parents' life. Not one. Ever."

But in '75 unfortunately when Ève came to Chile, she says, Ève found Hans Gunther fortunately they spoke together and he died three months later. So Ève came back to Chile. She invited her to live in Paris. And Inès followed her.

—Your father was the son of Andreas Jonas. He never spoke to you about his father?

—NEVER.

I concluded that he *said* to her, by force of a dead man's silence: I will never speak of my father.

It forms a name: Never NEVER. It's the name of the ghost of Andreas Jonas.

Inès quickly gives everything she has. I had a little book, she says: my father wrote in a notebook. In German I think. I didn't read it. If I find the thing, I'll send it to you. She says. She doesn't know German.

It occurs to me that Hans Gunther did not destroy this notebook. Inès did not throw it away. She found it. Perhaps the father didn't have time to think about it. Perhaps he had forgotten the notebook.

So, we think, all will not have been lost forever. When I read it, if this notebook reaches me, I will say nothing. Let us not tamper with Silence.

Figure 1: The Jonas house at 2 Nikolaiort in Osnabrück

Figure 2: Osnabrück Station, October 23, 1935; Andreas Jonas (first on the right) and his friend Gustav Stein (second from the left) say good-bye

Figure 3: They are leaving forever!

Figure 4: Young people together. An evening in Osnabrück. Ève is the second girl from the right.

Translations and References

The words drawn by Pierre Alechinsky

Kristall: Crystal

Erinnerung: Memory

Hiob: Job

Ekelhaft: Disgusting

Zuckerkrönchen: Little crown of sugar

Ariesierung: Aryanisation

Vertreibung: Expulsion

P. 127: Photographs of the *Stolpersteine* ("Stumbling blocks," created by the artist Gunter Demnig), installed on the sidewalk before 25 Friedrichstrasse, Osnabrück. © Annie-Joëlle Ripoll, 2015.

Notes

Translator's Preface

1. Jacques Derrida, foreword to Hélène Cixous, *Stigmata*, ed. and trans. Eric Prenowitz (New York: Routledge, 1998), ix.

2. Hélène Cixous, "The Laugh of the Medusa," trans. Keith Cohen and Paula Cohen, *Signs* 1, no. 4 (Summer 1976): 875–893.

3. *Le rire de la Méduse, et autres ironies* (Paris: Éditions Galilée, 2010), 30.

4. See *Selected Plays of Hélène Cixous*, ed. Eric Prenowitz (New York: Routledge, 2003).

5. Hélène Cixous, *Benjamin à Montaigne. Il ne faut pas le dire* (Paris: Éditions Galilée, 2001).

6. Hélène Cixous, *Osnabrück* (Paris: Éditions des femmes, 1999), 230; my trans.

7. "Here ends the book of Osnabrück, just in front of Mount Moriah. The book of Jerusalem had already begun" (125). Beyond this end, however, there is an "appendix," which begins "When, after the end of the book . . ." (129).

8. Hélène Cixous, *Correspondance avec le Mur* (Paris: Éditions Galilée, 2017).

Osnabrück Station to Jerusalem

1. [Hélène Cixous, *Osnabrück* (Paris: Des femmes, 1999), 229. —Trans.]

2. While waiting for the Jews, the City had a great Synagogue built, without god in the form of a hive to attract them, a virgin construction from the ashes of the Synagogue eliminated during the night of November 9–10, 1938.

3. [Cixous, *Osnabrück*, 229–230. —Trans.]

4. [Or "his fault"; the French grammar does not differentiate. —Trans.]

Hélène Cixous is the founder of the first Women's Studies program in France, at the University of Paris VIII. Since 1967, she has published more than fifty "fictions," as well as numerous works of criticism on literature and many essays on the visual arts. She has long been a collaborator with Ariane Mnouchkine at the Théâtre du Soleil, and a number of her plays have been published. Her many books include *"Coming to Writing" and Other Essays* and *The Portable Cixous*.

Eva Hoffman is the author of the bestselling memoir *Lost in Translation: A Life in a New Language*. Her other books include *Shtetl, after Such Knowledge: Memory, History, and the Legacy of the Holocaust* and two novels, *The Secret* and *Illuminations*.

Peggy Kamuf is Professor Emerita of French and Comparative Literature at the University of Southern California. Her books include *Book of Addresses*, which won the René Wellek Prize, and, most recently, *Literature and the Remains of the Death Penalty*.

CPSIA information can be obtained
at www.ICGtesting.com
Printed in the USA
JSHW031811010822
28773JS00002B/74